John Lyly's Midas: A Retelling

David Bruce

Published by David Bruce, 2022.

JOHN LYLY'S MIDAS: A RETELLING

First edition. November 8, 2022.

Copyright © 2022 David Bruce.

ISBN: 979-8215800683

Written by David Bruce.

Table of Contents

Dedication

Dedicated to Carl Eugene Bruce and Josephine Saturday Bruce

My father, Carl Eugene Bruce, died on 24 October 2013. He used to work for Ohio Power, and at one time, his job was to shut off the electricity of people who had not paid their bills. He sometimes would find a home with an impoverished mother and some children. Instead of shutting off their electricity, he would tell the mother that she needed to pay her bill or soon her electricity would be shut off. He would write on a form that no one was home when he stopped by because if no one was home he did not have to shut off their electricity.

The best good deed that anyone ever did for my father occurred after a storm that knocked down many power lines. He and other linemen worked long hours and got wet and cold. Their feet were freezing because water got into their boots and soaked their socks. Fortunately, a kind woman gave my father and the other linemen dry socks to wear.

My mother, Josephine Saturday Bruce, died on 14 June 2003. She used to work at a store that sold clothing. One day, an impoverished mother with a baby clothed in rags walked into the store and started shoplifting in an interesting way: The mother took the rags off her baby and dressed the infant in new clothing. My mother knew that this mother could not afford to buy the clothing, but she helped the mother dress her baby and then she watched as the mother walked out of the store without paying.

My mother and my father both died at 7:40 p.m.

Cover Photo for John Lyly's *Midas*: A Retelling:
Brett Hondow
https://pixabay.com/photos/coins-gold-golden-bounty-riches-1637722/

***

Educate Yourself
Read Like A Wolf Eats
Be Excellent to Each Other
Books Then, Books Now, Books Forever

***

In this retelling, as in all my retellings, I have tried to make the work of literature accessible to modern readers who may lack some of the knowledge about mythology, religion, and history that the literary work's contemporary audience had.

Do you know a language other than English? If you do, I give you permission to translate this book, copyright your translation, publish or self-publish it, and keep all the royalties for yourself. (Do give me credit, of course, for the original retelling.)

I would like to see my retellings of classic literature used in schools, so I give permission to the country of Finland (and all other countries) to buy (or get free) one copy of this book as an eBook and give copies to all students forever. I also give permission to the state of Texas (and all other states) to buy (or get free) one copy of this eBook and give copies to all students forever. I also give permission to all teachers to buy (or get free) one copy of this eBook and give copies to all students forever.

Teachers need not actually teach my retellings. Teachers are welcome to give students copies of my eBooks as background material. For example, if they are teaching Homer's *Iliad* and *Odyssey*, teachers are welcome to give students copies of my *Virgil's* Aeneid: *A Retelling in Prose* and tell students, "Here's another ancient epic you may want to read in your spare time."

CAST OF CHARACTERS

Prologue.

King Midas, King of Phrygia (now part of western Turkey).

Sophronia, Daughter of King Midas.

Counselors of King Midas: *Eristus. Martius. Mellacrites.*

Petulus, Page to Mellacrites.

Celia, Daughter of Mellacrites.

Pipenetta, Maid to Celia.

Licio, Page to Celia.

Minutius, another Page.

The gods: *Bacchus, god of wine. Apollo, aka Phoebus Apollo, aka Phoebus. Pan, god of the wild.*

Voice of Apollo's **Oracle.**

Shepherds: *Menalcas. Coryn. Celthus. Dryapon. Amyntas.*

Motto, a Barber.

Dello, his apprentice.

A **Huntsman.**

Erato, a Nymph, Priestess to Pan.

Other Nymphs, including *Thalia*.

Ladies of the Court: *Camilla. Amerula. Suavia.*

Scene: Phrygia and Delphi.

NOTES:

In this play, the island of Lesbos may stand for the island of Britain and especially the country of England. King Midas may stand for King Philip II of Spain. The King of Lesbos may stand for Queen Elizabeth I of England. At this time, Britain and Spain were enemies, and recently, in 1588, England had defeated the Spanish Armada.

King Midas is the King of Phrygia (now part of western Turkey). He is NOT King Minos of Crete, which is famous for the Minotaur and the Labyrinth it was kept in.

In this society, a person of higher rank would use "thou," "thee," "thine," and "thy" when referring to a person of lower rank. (These terms were also used affectionately and between equals.) A person of lower rank would use "you" and "your" when referring to a person of higher rank.

The word "wench" at this time was not necessarily negative. It was often used affectionately.

The word "fair" can mean attractive, beautiful, handsome, good-looking.

"Sirrah" was a title used to address someone of a social rank inferior to the speaker. Friends, however, could use it to refer to each other, and fathers could call their sons "sirrah."

THE PROLOGUE IN ST. PAUL'S

The Prologue said to you, the readers, all of whom are either men or honorary men:

"Gentlemen, so fickle and difficult to please is the world that for apparel there is no fashion, for music there is no instrument, for diet there is no delicacy, and for plays there is no invention except that which breeds satiety before noon, and contempt before night."

The Prologue spoke about the difficulty various service providers have in satisfying the public:

"Come to the tailor, he has gone to the painters to study fashion in paintings and learn how more cunning and skill may lurk in the fashion than can be expressed in the making."

Tailors did study paintings to see what fashions the figures were wearing.

The Prologue continued:

"Ask the musicians, they will say their heads ache with devising notes beyond Ela, a very high note.

"Inquire at ordinaries [taverns that serve food], there must be salads for the Italian; toothpicks for the Spaniard; pots of alcoholic beverages for the German; stews and porridges for the Englishman.

"At our theatrical performances, soldiers call for tragedies: Their object is blood.

"Courtiers call for comedies: Their subject is love.

"Countrymen call for pastorals: Shepherds are their saints.

"Trade and travel have woven the nature of all nations into ours; and they have made this land like arras, full of fanciful images, which formerly was broadcloth, full of workmanship."

An arras is a wall hanging in which are woven scenes and/or figures.

The Prologue continued:

"Time has mixed up our minds, and our minds have mixed up the matter; but all comes to this pass, that what heretofore has been served in several dishes for a feast, is now minced in a large plate for a gallimaufry [stew made from odds and ends of food]. If we present a mingle-mangle, our fault is to be excused, because the whole world has become a hodge-podge."

"Mingle-mangle" and "hodge-podge" both mean "mishmash."

The Prologue continued:

"We are anxious about your judgments because you are wise.

"We are anxious about our own performance because we are not perfect.

"We are anxious about our author's play because he is idle.

"Only this encourages us, that presenting our studies and play before gentlemen, even if they receive an inward mislike, we shall not be hissed with an open disgrace.

"*Stirps rudis urtica est; stirps generosa, rosa.*"

The Latin means: "A man of low birth is a nettle; a man of high birth is a rose."

CHAPTER 1

— 1.1 —

Bacchus, King Midas, Eristus, Martius, and Mellacrites met in the gardens before King Midas' palace.

Bacchus was the god of wine.

King Midas was the King of Phrygia (now part of western Turkey). He had been entertaining Bacchus.

Eristus, Martius, and Mellacrites were King Midas' counselors.

Bacchus said:

"King Midas, where the gods bestow benefits they ask thanks, but where they receive good turns, they give rewards.

"Thou have filled my belly with food, my ears with music, and my eyes with wonders.

"Bacchus of all the gods is the best fellow, and King Midas among men is a king of fellows."

A fellow is a convivialist: a good liver, someone fond of good food and good music and good sights and other good things, including good company.

Bacchus continued:

"All thy grounds are vineyards, and thy fruit are grapes; thy chambers are wine cellars, and thy household items are standing cups."

Standing cups are wine cups that have stems and bases they stand on.

Bacchus said:

"Therefore, ask me for anything, and it shall be granted.

"Would thou have the pipes of thy conduits to run wine, the udders of thy beasts to drop nectar, or thy trees to bud ambrosia?"

Nectar is the drink of the gods; ambrosia is the food of the gods.

Bacchus continued:

"Do thou desire to be fortunate in thy love, or famous in thy victories, or to have the years of thy life be as many as the hairs on thy head?"

Hmm. Be careful what you ask for, King Midas. Mythology has tales of mortals asking to live many, many years more than is normal, but forgetting to ask for endless youth. Such mortals grow older and older, and when one such mortal, a Sibyl, was asked what she wished for most, she wished for death.

Bacchus continued:

"Nothing shall be denied, so great is Bacchus, and so happy is King Midas."

King Midas replied:

"Bacchus, for a king to beg something from a god is no shame, but to ask with advice, is wisdom.

"Give me permission to consult my advisors, lest desiring things above my reach, I will be burnt with Phaeton, or desiring things against nature, I will be drowned with Icarus, and with us so perishing, the world shall both laugh and wonder, crying, *Magnis tamen excidit ausis.*"

The Latin means: "Yet at least he fell because of his deeds of great daring."

The Latin quotation is from Ovid, *Metamorphoses*, II.328.

Phaeton attempted to drive the Sun-chariot across the sky, but he could not manage the horses, and so it came close to Earth and would have set it on fire, but Jupiter, King of the gods, hurled a thunderbolt and killed Phaeton, who fell to Earth.

Daedalus and his son, Icarus, were imprisoned on the island of Crete. To escape imprisonment, Daedalus fashioned wings made out of wax and feathers so that they could fly away from the island where they were imprisoned. He warned his son not to fly too high, for if he did, the sun would melt the wax, the feathers would fall out of the wings, and he would fall into the sea and drown.

This is exactly what happened. Icarus became excited because he was flying, he flew too high, the wax of his wings melted, the feathers fell out of the wings, and he drowned.

Bacchus granted the permission that King Midas had requested: "Consult. Bacchus will consent."

King Midas said to his advisers, "Now, my lords, let me hear your opinions. What wish may make my days most happy and may make his subjects best content?"

Eristus expressed his opinion that King Midas ought to ask for love:

"If I were a king, I would wish to possess my mistress, for what sweetness can there be found in life, but love? The more mortal the wounds of love are to the heart, the more immortal they make the possessors.

"And who does not know that the possessing of love must be the most precious thing because the pursuing of it is so pleasing?"

Martius expressed his opinion that King Midas ought to ask for political and military power:

"Love is a pastime for children, breeding nothing but folly, and nourishing nothing but idleness. I would wish to be monarch of the world, conquering kingdoms like villages and being the greatest on the earth. I would wish to be commander of the whole earth.

"For what is there that more tickles the mind of a king than a hope to be the only king, wringing out of every country tribute, and in his own country to sit in triumph? Those who call conquerors ambitious, are like those who call thrift 'covetousness,' call cleanliness 'pride,' and call honesty 'preciseness' or 'severe Puritanical fastidiousness.'

"Command the world, King Midas. A greater thing you cannot desire, a lesser thing you should not."

"What do you say, Mellacrites?" King Midas asked.

Mellacrites expressed his opinion that King Midas ought to ask for gold:

"Nothing, except that these two have said nothing.

"I would wish that everything I touched might turn to gold because gold is the sinews of war, and gold is the sweetness of peace.

"Isn't it gold that makes the most chaste to yield to lust, the most honest and loyal to yield to lewdness, the wisest to yield to folly, the most faithful to yield to deceit, and the most holy in heart to be most hollow of heart?"

Gold can buy a lot of flesh and corrupt a lot of character.

Mellacrites continued:

"In this word 'gold' are all the powers of the gods, the desires of men, the wonders of the world, the miracles of nature, the generosity of fortune and triumphs of time.

"By the use of gold, you may shake the courts of other princes, and have your own settled.

"One spade of gold undermines faster than a hundred mattocks of steel."

Mattocks are digging implements. One way to undermine the walls of a city is to dig tunnels under the walls and then set off explosives. A quicker way is to bribe people to open the gates and let in your soldiers.

Mellacrites continued:

"Would one be thought religious and devout?

"*Quantum quisque sua nummorum servat in arca, tantum habet et fidei*: Religion's weighing scales are golden bags."

The Latin means: "Every man is trusted in proportion to the amount of money he has in his treasury."

The Latin quotation is from Juvenal, *Satires*, III.143-144.

Mellacrites continued:

"Do you desire virtue?

"*Quaerenda pecunia primum est, virtus post nummos*: The first stair of virtue is money."

The Latin means: "Seek money first; seek virtue after you have money."

The Latin quotation comes from Horace, *Epistles*, I.1.53-54.

Mellacrites continued:

"Does anyone thirst to enter the rank of the gentry and become a gentleman, and does anyone wish to be esteemed beautiful?

"*Et genus et formam regina pecunia donat*: King Coin has a mint to stamp gentlemen, and it has the art, aka skill, to make amiableness."

"Amiable" means "worthy to be loved."

The Latin means: "Queen Pecunia [Queen Money] gives both pedigree and beauty."

The Latin quotation comes from Horace, *Epistles*, I.6.37.

Mellacrites continued:

"I don't deny that love is sweet, and I don't deny that love is the marrow of a man's mind.

"I don't deny that to conquer kings is the quintessence of the thoughts of kings.

"Why, then get both with gold:

"*Aurea sunt vero nunc aecula, plurimus auro venit honos, auro conciliatur amor*: It is a world for gold; honor and love are both obtained through the payment of interest."

The Latin means: "Now is the Golden Age. The greatest honor is sold for gold; love is sold for gold."

The Latin quotation comes from Ovid, *Ars Amatoria*, II.277-278, but Ovid has *vere*, not *vero*.

Mellacrites continued:

"Does King Midas determine to tempt the minds of his enemy's true subjects? Does King Midas determine to draw them from obedience to treachery, from their allegiance and oaths to treason and perjury?

"*Quid non mortalia pectora cogit auri sacra fames?* What holes does gold not bore in men's hearts?"

The Latin means: "What doesn't this insatiable love of gold compel mortal men to do?"

The Latin quotation comes from Virgil, *Aeneid*, III.56-57.

Mellacrites continued:

"Such virtue is there in gold that although it is bred in the most barren ground, and trodden under foot, it mounts to sit on princes' heads."

Gold is used in crowns.

Mellacrites continued:

"Wish for gold, King Midas, or wish not to be King Midas.

"In the counsel of the gods, wasn't Anubis with his long nose of gold preferred before Neptune, whose statue was only brass?

"And wasn't Aesculapius more honored for his golden beard than Apollo was honored for his sweet harmony?"

Lucian wrote the *Zeus Tragoedus*, in which the gods were seated according to the material their statue was made of, rather than according to their merit and virtue. Anubis' statue had a long nose of gold, and so he was seated in a more prestigious seat than Neptune. Anubis is often portrayed as a man with a dog's head.

Aesculapius' statue had a gold beard, and he was seated in a more prestigious seat than Apollo. Aesculapius is the god of medicine.

Eristus said, "To have gold and not love (which cannot be purchased by gold) is to be a slave to gold."

Martius said, "To possess mountains of gold, and a mistress more precious than gold, and not to command the world, is to make King Midas a new apprentice to a money-coining mint, and a journeyman to a woman."

A journeyman is a hired man.

Mellacrites said:

"To enjoy a fair lady in love, and lack fair gold to give, and to have thousands of people to fight, and no penny to pay — will make one's mistress wild and will make his soldiers tame.

"Jupiter was a god, but he knew gold was a greater god: and he flew into those grates with his golden wings, where he could not enter with his swan's wings."

Jupiter lusted after the mortal maiden Danae. The gods are shape-shifters, and Jupiter assumed the form of a shower of gold, passed through the grates of the walls imprisoning her, and impregnated her. She gave birth to the hero Perseus.

A cynical interpretation of the myth is that Jupiter gained access to Danae by giving her jailer a shower of gold coins.

In one of his shape-shifting adventures, Jupiter assumed the form of a swan and impregnated Leda, who gave birth to Helen, who later became Helen of Troy, and to Clytemnestra, who married and later murdered Agamemnon, leader of the Greek forces against Troy.

Mellacrites continued:

"What stayed Atalanta's course with Hippomenes? An apple of gold."

Atalanta, who was wooed by many men, wished to preserve her virginity. Being swift, she challenged her suitors to a foot race. If she won the foot race, she would remain unmarried. If a suitor won the footrace, she would marry that suitor. For a long time, she remained a virgin, but Venus, the goddess of sexual passion, helped Hippomenes to win the foot race. She gave him three golden apples, and during the foot race, he threw the golden apples, one at a time, off the direct path to the finish line. Atalanta picked up the golden apples, and this slowed her down enough that Hippomenes won the race and married her.

Mellacrites continued:

"What made the three goddesses strive? An apple of gold."

Peleus was the human man who married the minor sea-goddess Thetis and who fathered Achilles. Obviously, you do not want discord at a wedding, and therefore, Eris, goddess of discord, was not invited to the wedding feast of Peleus and Thetis. Even though Eris was not invited to the wedding feast, she showed up anyway and she threw an apple on a table at the wedding feast. Inscribed on the apple was the phrase "For the fairest." Three goddesses claimed the apple, meaning that each of the three goddesses thought that she was the fairest, or most beautiful:

Hera was the wife of Jupiter, King of the gods. Her Roman name is Juno.

Athena was the goddess of wisdom. Her Roman name is Minerva.

Aphrodite was the goddess of sexual passion. Her Roman name is Venus.

Paris was a prince of Troy, and Jupiter allowed him to judge the three goddesses' beauty contest.

Each of the goddesses offered Paris a bribe if he would choose her:

Hera offered Paris political power: several cities he could rule.

Athena offered Paris prowess in battle. Paris could become a mighty and feared warrior.

Paris chose Aphrodite, who had offered him the most beautiful woman in the world to be his wife, as the victor of the beauty contest. That woman turned out to be Helen, the wife of King Menelaus of Sparta. She became Helen of Troy, and the Trojan War was fought over her.

Mellacrites continued:

"If therefore thou don't make thy mistress a goldfinch, thou may perhaps find her a wagtail. Believe me, *Res est ingeniosa dare*."

The Latin means: "The clever act is to give."

The Latin quotation comes from Ovid, *Amores*, I.8.62.

Mellacrites continued:

"Besides, how many gates of cities this golden key has opened we may remember of late, and ought to fear hereafter.

"That iron world is worn out, and the golden age has now come."

Some ancients believed that the world was steadily growing worse. The golden age came first, then it was followed by the silver age, the bronze age, the heroic age, and the iron age.

According to Mellacrites, because of men's love of gold, this is the golden age.

Mellacrites continued:

"*Sub Jove nunc mundus, iussa sequare Jovis.*"

The Latin means: "Under Jove the world now is; we must follow the orders of Jove."

"Jove" is Jupiter, King of the gods.

Eristus said, "Gold is just the guts of the earth."

Mellacrites said:

"I would rather have the earth's guts than the moon's brains — that is, than be a lunatic.

"What is it that gold cannot command, or has not conquered?

"Justice herself, who sits wimpled — blindfolded — about the eyes, wears the blindfold not because she will take no gold, but because she would not be seen blushing when she takes it. The scales she holds are not to weigh the right of the cause, but the weight of the bribe; she will put away her naked sword if thou offer her a golden scabbard."

A wimple is a nun's headdress.

King Midas said to his advisors:

"Stop arguing. I have made my decision."

He then said to Bacchus:

"It is gold, Bacchus, that King Midas desires. Let everything that King Midas touches be turned to gold, so shall thou bless thy guest, and manifest thy godhead.

"Let it be gold, Bacchus."

Bacchus said, "King Midas, thy wish cleaves to thy last word. Pick up this stone."

King Midas picked up the stone, which turned to gold.

He said, "Fortunate King Midas! It is gold, Mellacrites! Gold! It is gold!"

"Hold this stick," Mellacrites said, handing him a stick.

King Midas held the stick, which turned to gold.

"It is gold, Mellacrites!" King Midas said. "My sweet boy, all is gold! Forever honored be Bacchus, who above measure has made King Midas fortunate."

Bacchus said:

"If King Midas is pleased, Bacchus is pleased. I will go to my temple with Silenus, for by this time there are many to offer to me sacrifices."

Silenus was Bacchus' traveling companion. He was a continually drunk and continually jovial Satyr: half-man, half goat.

Bacchus then said:

"*Poenam pro munere poscis.*"

The Latin means: "You have asked for a punishment instead of a gift."

The Latin quotation is from Ovid, *Metamorphoses*, II.99.

The Sun-god said that to Phaeton when Phaeton asked to drive the Sun-chariot across the sky.

Bacchus exited.

King Midas said:

"Come, my lords, I will pave my court with gold, and I will deck my turrets with gold, and these petty islands near Phrygia shall totter, and other kingdoms shall be turned topsy-turvy.

"I will command both the affections and the fortunes of men.

"Chastity will grow cheap where gold is thought dear. Celia, chaste Celia, shall yield."

Celia was the daughter of Mellacrites, who was present, and who had advised King Midas to ask that everything he touched turn to gold.

Power corrupts. Wealth can be a kind of power.

King Midas continued:

"You, my lords, shall have my hands in your houses, turning your brazen gates to fine gold. Thus, King Midas shall be monarch of the world, the darer of fortune, the commander of love.

"Come, let us go inside."

Mellacrites said, "We follow, desiring that our thoughts may be touched with thy fingers, so that they also may become gold."

Eristus said, "Well, I fear the outcome of this wish because of Bacchus' last words: '*Poenam pro munere poscis*.'"

King Midas said, "Tush, he is a drunken god, or else he would not have given so great a gift. Now that it is done, I don't care about anything he can do."

Petulus and Licio talked together. Petulus was a page to Mellacrites, and Licio was a page to Celia. Mellacrites was a counselor to King Midas, and Celia was his daughter.

Licio asked Petulus, "Thou serve Mellacrites, and I serve Celia, his daughter, so which of us is the better man?"

Petulus responded, "The masculine gender is more worthy than the feminine; therefore, Licio, backare."

In other words: I serve a man, and you serve a woman, so I am the better man. Therefore, back off, and give place to me.

Licio said, "That is when those two genders are in conflict, but when they belong both to one thing, then —"

Petulus interrupted, "— what then?"

"Then they agree like the fiddle and the stick," Licio said.

They play beautiful music together.

Petulus said:

"*Pulchrè sane*! God's blessing on thy blue nose!"

Pulchrè sane is Latin for "very nice."

Veins showing through the skin look blue. They are often taken as evidence of fragility or refinement.

Licio's "they agree like the fiddle and the stick" was mildly suggestive. Someone such as Petulus would speak words that were much more than suggestive.

Petulus continued:

"But Licio, my mistress — Celia — is a proper woman."

In this context, a "mistress" is a female boss.

A "proper" woman is 1) good-looking, and/or 2) respectable.

"Aye, but thou don't know her properties," Licio said.

"I don't care about her qualities, as long as I may embrace her quantity," Petulus said.

Her quantity is her body.

"Are you so pert?" Licio asked.

"Pert" can mean saucy and impertinent.

"Aye, and I am so ex*pert* that I can as well tell the thoughts of a woman's heart by her eyes as I can tell the change of the weather by an almanac," Petulus said.

Telling the change of the weather by an almanac doesn't always work. It's much better to look out the window.

"Sir boy, you must not be saucy," Licio said.

"No, I mustn't, but I ought to be faithful and serviceable," Petulus said.

"Lock up your lips, or I will lop them off," Licio said. "But sirrah, for thy better instructions I will unfold every wrinkle and trick of my mistress' disposition."

"Please do," Petulus said.

"But for this time, I will only handle the head and the purtenance — the head and that which pertains to it," Licio said.

"Nothing else?" Petulus asked.

"Why, won't that be a long hour's work to describe that which is almost a whole day's work to dress?" Licio asked.

Women can take a long time to dress, even with help from servants.

"Proceed," Petulus said.

Licio began to describe Celia's head:

"First, she has a head as round as a tennis ball."

"I wish my bed were a hazard," Petulus said.

He wished that his bed was hazardous to young unmarried virgins.

The *Oxford English Dictionary* defines a "hazard" in Real Tennis as "Each of the various openings or galleries around a court, *spec.* those which are not winning openings."

Tennis balls can be hit into hazards.

"Why?" Licio asked.

"Nothing, except that I would have her head there among other balls," Petulus said.

Hmm. Indelicate, that.

Licio said:

"*Video, pro intelligo.*"

The Latin means: "I see, for I understand."

Licio continued:

"Then she has a hawk's eye."

A hawk's eyes could be seeled — sewn shut — as part of its training. Celia's eyes would have to be sewn shut if her head was to come anywhere near Petulus' balls.

"O, I wish that I were a partridge head," Petulus said.

"To what end?" Licio said. "Why?"

"So that she might tire with her eyes on my countenance," Petulus said.

Falcons would "tire" — that is, tear — flesh. Petulus wanted Celia to feast her eyes on his face.

But "tire" can also mean "become fatigued," so Petulus was also unintentionally saying that he wanted Celia to become tired of looking at his face.

"Would thou be hanged for that?" Licio asked.

One way for Celia to tire — to feast — with her eyes on Petulus' countenance would be for the two to be close together, paying close attention to what the other said. If that were to happen, they would be "hanging" on each other's lips.

Petulus answered, "*Scilicet.*"

The Latin means, "Of course."

Of course, if Petulus were to "annoy" Celia sexually, she could "tire" — tear — his face, and he could be hung.

"Well, she has the tongue of a parrot," Licio said.

"To have a black tongue in a fair mouth is like having a dagger made out of lead in a velvet sheath," Petulus said.

"Tush, her having the tongue of a parrot is not for the blackness, but for the babbling, for every hour she will cry, 'Walk, knave, walk,'" Licio said.

Parrots were frequently taught these words. Possibly, the joke was that the parrot would say them to someone who was NOT a knave and did NOT want to be called a knave.

"Then I will mutter, 'A rope for parrot, a rope,'" Petulus said.

The word "rope" was often taught to parrots. This word referred to 1) the hangman's noose, and 2) (possibly) a rope perch for the parrot.

Licio said:

"So may thou be hanged, not by the lips, but by the neck.

"Then, sir, she has a calf's tooth."

"O monstrous mouth!" Petulus said. "I wish then it had been a sheep's eye, and a neat's — a cow's — tongue."

"It is not for the bigness, but the sweetness," Licio said. "All her teeth are as sweet as the sweet tooth of a calf."

"Sweetly meant," Petulus said.

"She has the ears of a want," Licio said.

A "want" is a mole, which this society thought to have very good hearing despite this society's believing that moles have no ears.

"Does she want — lack — ears?" Petulus asked.

"I say the ears of a want, a mole," Licio said. "Thou lack the wit and intelligence to understand me. She will hear although she is ever so low on the ground."

"Why, then if someone would ask her a question, it is likely she will hearken to it," Petulus said.

The questions these two servants were likely to ask her were propositions.

Licio said:

"Hearken thou after that."

In other words: Give it a try.

Licio continued:

"She has the nose of a sow."

"Then it is likely she wears her wedding ring there," Petulus said.

"No, she can smell a knave a mile off," Licio said.

Her ability to smell knaves kept her from marrying knaves.

"Let us go farther, Licio, for she has both of us in the wind," Petulus said. "She can smell both of us."

"Farther" can mean 1) farther away, or 2) farther in our conversation.

"She has a beetle brow," Licio said.

A beetle brow can be bushy eyebrows or frowning eyebrows.

"What, is she beetle browed?" Petulus asked.

"Thou have a beetle head!" Licio said. "Thou are a blockhead. I say the brow of a beetle, a little fly, whose brow is as black as velvet."

"What kind of lips has she?" Petulus asked.

"Tush, the lips are no part of the head; they are only made for a double-leaf door for the mouth," Licio said.

"Tush" means "bah."

"What is then the chin?" Petulus asked.

"That is only the threshold to the door," Licio said.

Petulus said:

"I perceive you are driven to the wall that stands behind the door — that is, I see that you are driven to your last extremity, for this is ridiculous.

"But now that you can say no more of the head, begin with the purtenances, for that was your promise."

"Purtenances" are accessories.

Licio said:

"The purtenances! It is impossible to count them up, much less to tell the nature of them.

"These accessories include:

"Hoods.

"Frontlets: ornaments or bands worn on the forehead.

"Wires, aka wire frameworks for holding up hairstyles.

"Caules, aka nets or small caps for the hair.

"Curling-irons.

"Periwigs, aka wigs.

"Bodkins, aka pins for pinning up hair.

"Fillets, aka ribbons or bands for tying up hair.

"Hair laces, aka strings for tying up hair.

"Ribbons.

"Rolls, aka cushions that form part of a headdress.

"Knotstrings, aka ribbons or strings used to make bows.

"Glasses, aka mirrors.

"Combs.

"Caps.

"Hats.

"Coifs, aka close-fitting caps that are tied under the chin.

"Kerchers, aka kerchiefs.

"Cloths, aka veils.

"Earrings.

"Borders, aka ornamental borders on the edge of a hat or a piece of clothing.

"Crippins, aka hair nets.

"Shadows."

The *Oxford English Dictionary* gives this as one of its definitions of "shadow": "A woman's headdress, or a portion of a headdress, projecting forward so as to shade the face."

Licio continued:

"Spots, aka beauty spots.

"And so many other trifles that I lack the words of art to name them, the time to utter them, and the wit to remember them. These are only a few notes."

"Notes, you say?" Petulus said. "I note one thing."

"What is that?" Licio asked.

"That if every part of a woman requires as much as the head, it will make the richest husband in the world ache at the heart," Petulus said.

And ache in the wallet.

Celia's handmaid, Pipenetta, entered the scene.

Licio said:

"But wait, here comes Pipenetta."

He then asked her:

"What is the news?"

"I would not be in your coats for anything," Pipenetta said.

"Indeed, if thou should rig — should romp — up and down in our jackets, thou would be thought a complete tomboy," Licio said.

"I mean I would not be in your cases," Pipenetta said.

By "cases," Pipenetta meant "positions," but the word can also mean "clothes" or "skins."

"Neither shall thou, Pipenetta, for first, they are too little for thy body, and then they are too fair to pull over so foul a skin," Petulus said.

"These boys are drunk!" Pipenetta said. "I would not be in your takings."

"Takings" can mean "circumstances" or "situations."

"I think so, for we take nothing in our hands but weapons," Licio said. "It is for thee to use needles and pins, a sampler and not a buckler."

A sampler is a piece of embroidery, and a buckler is a shield.

"Nay, then, we shall never have done!" Pipenetta said. "I mean I would not be so curst as you shall be."

Pipenetta meant "so damned with curses," but Petulus deliberately misunderstood the word to be "coursed," which means "hunted."

"Worse and worse!" Petulus said. "We are no chase (pretty mops), for deer we are not, neither red nor fallow, because we are bachelors and we don't have *cornu copia*. We lack heads."

"Mops" is a term of endearment that refers to a girl or woman.

"Red" and "fallow" are species of deer.

A *cornucopia* is a horn of plenty, but Petulus was also using "horn" to mean the antlers of deer and the invisible horns that were said to grow on the heads of husbands with unfaithful wives.

Petulus continued:

"Hares we cannot be, because they are male one year, and the next year they are female. We don't change our sex."

People have had many odd beliefs about animals through the centuries.

Petulus continued:

"We are not badgers, for our legs are one as long as the other."

The front legs of badgers are powerful and strongly built. It can seem as if their front legs are longer than their back legs.

Petulus continued:

"And who will take us to be foxes, we who stand so near a goose and don't bite?"

A goose is a fool. Petulus was referring to Pipenetta.

Pipenetta said, "Fools you are, and therefore good game for wise men to hunt, but I leave you knaves for honest wenches — honest women — to talk about."

"Nay, stay, sweet Pipenetta, we are just disposed to be merry," Licio said.

Pipenetta said:

"I marvel how old you will be before you are disposed to be honest.

"But this is the matter at hand:

"My master has gone abroad, and he wants his page to wait on him.

"And my mistress would rise, and she wants your worship to fetch her hair."

"Her hair" is her wig.

"Why, isn't it on her head?" Petulus joked.

"I think it should be, but I mean the hair that she must wear today," Pipenetta said.

"Why, does she wear any hair except her own?" Licio asked.

Pipenetta said:

"In faith, sir, no, I am sure it's her own when she pays for it.

"But have you heard the strange news at the court?"

"No, unless it is this: to have one's hair lie all night out of the house away from one's head," Petulus said.

"Tush!" Pipenetta said. "The news is that everything that King Midas touches is gold."

"The devil it is!" Petulus said.

"Indeed, gold is the devil," Pipenetta said.

"Thou are deceived, wench, angels are gold," Licio said. "But is it true?"

"Angels" are gold coins.

"True?" Pipenetta said. "Why the food that he touches turns to gold, so does the drink, and so does his clothing."

"I wish that he would give me a good box — a good blow — on the ear, so that I might have a golden cheek," Petulus said.

Licio said:

"How happy we shall be if he would but stroke our heads, so that we might have golden hairs.

"But let us all go in, lest he lose the virtue — the power — of the gift before we taste the benefit."

"If he takes a cudgel — a stick or rod — it turns to gold, yet when he beats you with it, you shall only feel the weight of gold," Pipenetta said. "You shall not turn to gold."

"What is the difference between to be beaten with gold, and to be beaten gold?" Petulus asked.

Gold can be shaped by repeatedly beating — striking — it. Then it is beaten gold.

"As much difference as to say, drink before you go, and go before you drink," Pipenetta said.

"Come, let us go, lest we drink from a dry cup and get no benefit because of our long tarrying and lingering," Licio said.

They exited.

CHAPTER 2

— 2.1 —

Eristus and Celia talked together. Eristus was one of King Midas' counselors. Celia was the daughter of Mellacrites, another of King Midas' counselors. Eristus was in love with Celia.

"Fair Celia, thou see of gold there is satiety, but of love there cannot be satiety," Eristus said.

Because of King Midas' "gift," there was an abundance of gold in his kingdom. There was, however, not an abundance of love, according to Eristus; after all, Celia did not love Eristus.

Celia said, "If thou should wish that whatsoever thou thought might be love, as King Midas wished that whatever he touched might be gold, it may be that love would be as loathsome to thine ears as gold is to his eyes and love would make thy heart pinch with melancholy, as his guts do with famine."

King Midas had discovered the downside of his wish: He was starving because all the food he touched turned to gold before he could eat it.

"No, sweet Celia, in love there is variety," Eristus said.

"Indeed, men vary and are fickle in their love," Celia said.

She meant that men are fickle and change the person whom they choose to love. They go from woman to woman.

"They vary their love, yet they do not change it," Eristus said.

"Love and change are at variance and in conflict; therefore, if they vary, they must change," Celia said.

Eristus said, "Men change the manner of their love, not the humor, aka inclination to love; men change the means how to obtain their love, not the mistress they honor. So did Jupiter, who could not entreat Danae by golden words. He possessed his love by means of a golden shower. He did not alter his affection for Danae, but he did use a different art to get what he wanted."

Celia said:

"The same Jupiter was an eagle, a swan, a bull; and for every saint he had a new shape, as men have for every mistress a new shadow."

"A new shadow" is a new guise. Men change their personalities to get women.

Jupiter was a horny god who pursued women, whether or not they wanted to be pursued. Many women wanted to pursue their virginity: They were saints.

Celia continued:

"If you take the example of the gods, who is more wanton, more wavering than the gods?"

Disguised as an eagle, Jupiter kidnapped the beautiful boy Ganymede, who became his cupbearer, and, some say, his catamite. A catamite is a boy kept as a sexual object for a homosexual man.

Disguised as a swan, Jupiter seduced Leda, who bore him two daughters: Helen, who later became known as Helen of Troy, and Clytemnestra, who married and later murdered Agamemnon, leader of the Greek forces against the Trojans.

Disguised as a bull, Jupiter kidnapped the Phoenician woman Europa, who climbed on his back. He then swam to Crete, where Europa bore him a son: King Midas.

Jupiter slept with many, many mortal women and immortal goddesses. In Book 14 of Homer's *Iliad*, his wife sleeps with him so that he will fall asleep and the Greeks will fight well for a while. (Jupiter has been making sure that the Trojans fight well.) Overcome with lust for Hera, his wife, Jupiter mentions seven women and goddesses whom he has had sex with, and he mentions children that they have borne for him. The catalog of women and goddesses he has slept with is often called the "Leporello catalog." It is named after a famous aria in Mozart's *Don Giovanni*. Don Giovanni is better known by the name Don Juan.

Celia continued:

"If you take the example of yourselves, who are just men, who will think you are more constant and loyal than the gods?

"Eristus, if gold could have allured my eyes, thou know King Midas, who commands all things to be gold, would have conquered and won me.

"If threats might have made my heart afraid, King Midas, being a king, might have commanded my affections.

"If love, gold, or authority might have enchanted me, King Midas would have obtained what he wanted from me by love, gold, and authority.

*"Quorum si singula nostrum flectere non poterant, potuissent omnia mentem."*****

The Latin means: "If each of these things could not persuade me, all of them together might have succeeded."

Yes, they might have, but they didn't.

Earlier, King Midas had said, "Chastity will grow cheap where gold is thought dear. Celia, chaste Celia, shall yield."

Celia had not yielded.

The Latin quotation is adapted from Ovid, *Metamorphoses*, IX.608-609. Ovid used *duram* instead of *nostrum*.

Eristus said:

"Ah, Celia, if kings say they love and yet dissemble, who will dare to say that they dissemble, and not love? They command the affections of others to yield, and their own to be believed.

"My tears, which have made furrows in my cheeks and have made fountains in my eyes ...

"My sighs, which have made of my heart a furnace, and kindled in my head flames ...

"My body that melts by piecemeal, a little at a time, and my mind that pines and loses vitality at an instant ...

"All of these may witness that my love is both unspotted and pure, and that it is unspeakable and indescribable.

"Quorum si singula duram flectere non poterant, deberent, omnia mentem." *****

The Latin means: "If each of these things could not move your hard mind, all of them together should have succeeded."

Eristus then said:

"But wait, here comes the princess, with the rest of the lords."

Sophronia, Mellacrites, Martius, and other courtiers entered the scene. Sophronia was King Midas' daughter.

People were criticizing Mellacrites because of his advice to King Midas to ask Bacchus for a golden touch: that everything he touched would turn to gold.

Sophronia said:

"Mellacrites, I cannot tell whether I should more mislike thy counsel, or King Midas' consent, but I both condemn and wonder at your covetous humor — your greedy disposition.

"A greedy disposition is unfit for a king, whose honor should consist in liberality, not greediness; and a greedy disposition is unworthy the calling of Mellacrites, whose fame should rise by the soldiers' god, Mars, and not by the merchants' god, Gold."

Mellacrites replied:

"Madam, things past cannot be recalled, but they can be repented; and therefore, they are rather to be pitied than punished.

"It now behooves us how to redress the miserable condition of our king, not to dispute about the cause.

"Your highness sees, and without grief you cannot see, that his food turns to heavy gold in his mouth, and his wine slides down his throat like liquid gold. If he touches his robes, they are turned to gold, and what isn't there that touches him, but becomes gold?"

Eristus said, "Aye, Mellacrites, if thy tongue had been turned to gold before thou gave our king such counsel, King Midas' heart would have been full of ease, and thy mouth would have been full of gold."

Martius said:

"If my advice had taken place, King Midas, who now sits over head and ears in crowns [gold coins], would have worn upon his head many kings' crowns [diadems], and he who now is commander of dross would have been conqueror of the world."

"Dross" is something worthless. It literally is what is left over after gold is refined.

Martius continued:

"That greediness of Mellacrites, whose heart-strings are made of Plutus' purse-strings, has made King Midas, who should be a god on earth, a lump of earth."

Plutus is the god of wealth.

Martius continued:

"And thy effeminate mind, Eristus, whose eyes are stitched on Celia's face, and whose thoughts are gyved — fettered — to her beauty, has bred in all the court such a tender wantonness, that nothing is thought of but love, a passion proceeding from beastly lust, and colored with — that is, disguised by — a courtly name of love.

"Thus, while we follow the nature of things, we forget the names. Since this unsatiable thirst for gold, and this untemperate humor — intemperate desire — for lust has crept into the king's court, soldiers have begged alms from artificers and craftsmen, and with their helmet on their head, they have been glad to imitate a lover with a glove in his hat, which so much abates the courage of true captains that they must account it more honorable in the court to be a coward, as long as he is rich and amorous, than in a camp to be valiant, if he is poor and maimed."

The glove in a lover's hat is a gift from a lady.

Martius continued:

"He who pricks his finger with his mistress' needle is more favored than he who breaks his lance on his enemy's face, and he who has his mouth full of fair words is more favored than he who has his body full of deep scars.

"If one is old, and has silver hairs on his beard, as long as he has golden ruddocks — that is, gold coins — in his bags, he must be wise and honorable.

"If he is young and has curled locks on his head, amorous glances with his eyes, and smooth and flattering speeches in his mouth, then every lady's lap shall be his pillow, every lady's face his mirror, every lady's ear a sheath for his flatteries.

"True soldiers, if they are old, must beg in their own countries; if they are young, they must try the fortune of wars in another country."

Currently, there was no need for true soldiers in King Midas' country. So said Martius.

Martius continued:

"He is considered a man, who being let blood, carries his arm in a scarf of his mistress' favor. He is not considered a man, who bears his leg on a crutch for his country's safety."

In this society, blood-letting was a recognized medical procedure.

Sophronia said:

"Stop, Martius, although I know love to grow to such looseness, and hoarding of gold to such misery, and although I may rather grieve at both, than remedy either, yet thy animating and inspiring my father to continual arms, to conquer crowns, has only brought him into imminent danger of his own head.

"The love he has followed — I fear is unnatural.

"The riches he has got — I know are unmeasurable.

"The wars he has levied — I fear are unlawful.

"My father's love of riches and war has drawn his body with gray hairs to the grave's mouth; and his mind with eating cares to desperate determinations."

King Midas had been using his gold to hire soldiers.

Sophronia continued:

"Ambition has only two steps: The lowest step is blood, and the highest step is malicious envy.

"Both of these my unhappy father has climbed, digging mines of gold with the lives of men, and he is now maliciously envied and disliked by the whole world. He is surrounded with enemies round about the world, not knowing that Ambition has one heel nailed in hell, although she stretches her finger to touch the heavens.

"I wish the gods would remove this punishment, so that King Midas would be penitent.

"Let him thrust thee away and exile thee, Eristus, with thy love, into Italy, where they honor lust for a god, as the Egyptians did dogs.

"Let him thrust thee away and exile thee, Mellacrites, with thy greediness of gold, to the utmost parts of the west, Central and South America, where all the guts of the earth are gold.

"And let him thrust thee away and exile thee, Martius, who speak of nothing except blood and terror, into those barbarous nations, where nothing is to be found except blood and terror.

"Let Phrygia be an example of chastity, not lust.

"Let Phrygia be an example of liberality and generosity, not covetousness.

"Let Phrygia be an example of valor, not tyranny.

"I don't wish your bodies banished, but your minds, so that my father and your king may be our honor and the world's wonder.

"And thou, Celia, and all you ladies, learn this from Sophronia, that beauty in a minute is both a blossom and a blast — a blight.

"Love is a worm that, seeming to live in the eye, dies in the heart.

"You are all young, and fair; endeavor all of you to be wise and virtuous, so that when, like roses, you shall fall from the stalk, you may be gathered and distilled."

The distillation of roses results in rose oil, which is used in perfumes.

"Madam, I am free from love, and unfortunate to be beloved," Celia said.

She meant she was unfortunate to be loved by Eristus.

"To be free from love is strange, but to think being beloved is worthy of scorn is monstrous," Eristus said.

Sophronia said:

"Eristus, thy tongue itches to talk about love, and my ears tingle to hear it.

"I order you all, if you owe any duty to your king, to go immediately to the temple of Bacchus and offer praise-gifts and sacrifice, so that King Midas may be released of his wish, or his life. This I entreat you; this King Midas commands you.

"Don't argue with yourselves.

"Agree as one body to do this for your king, if ever you regarded King Midas as your lawful king."

"Madam, we will go, and we will omit nothing that duty may perform, or pains may perform," Mellacrites said.

Sophronia said:

"Go speedily, lest King Midas die before you return.

"And you, Celia, shall go with me, so that with talk we may beguile the time, and my father shall think of no food."

"I attend on you," Celia said.

They exited.

Licio, Petulus, and Pipenetta talked together in the garden before King Midas' palace. Petulus was a page to Mellacrites, and Licio was a page to Celia. Pipenetta was Celia's handmaiden.

"Ah, my girl, isn't this a golden world?" Licio asked Pipenetta.

"It is all the same as if it were lead with me, and yet as golden with me as with the king," Pipenetta said, "for I see it, and I don't feel it; he feels it, and he doesn't enjoy it. "

Pipenetta could see the gold, but she couldn't get her hands on any of it.

"Gold is just the earth's garbage, a weed bred by the sun, the very rubbish of barren ground," Licio said.

"Tush, Licio, thou are unlettered," Petulus said. "All the earth is an egg: The white is silver, and the yolk is gold."

"Tush" mean "Bah!"

"Why, thou fool, what hen would lay that egg?" Licio said.

"I warrant a goose did," Pipenetta said.

A "goose" is a fool.

"Nay, I believe a bull did," Licio said.

One meaning of "bull," according to the *Oxford English Dictionary*, is "A ludicrous jest."

"Blurt to you both!" Petulus said. "It was laid by the sun."

"Blurt" means "Bah!"

"The sun is rather a cock than a hen," Pipenetta said.

Helios, the Sun-god, was male. So was Apollo, who in Roman mythology drives the Sun-chariot across the sky. Helios and Apollo were sometimes conflated in mythology.

"It is true, girl, else how could Titan have trodden Daphne?" Licio said.

The Titans Hyperion and Theia were the parents of Helios, and so Helios was called here a Titan. Apollo, however, was the god who pursued Daphne. Apollo loved Daphne, but Daphne did not love Apollo, and so she fled from him. He trod in her footprints and followed her. Daphne prayed to her father, a river-god, and she was transformed into a bay laurel tree, which became sacred to Apollo.

"I weep over both your wits!" Petulus said. "If I prove in every respect that there is no difference between an egg and gold, won't you then grant that gold is an egg?"

"Yes, but I believe thy idle imagination will make it an addled egg — a rotten egg," Pipenetta said.

Yes. And addled logic.

"Let us hear," Licio said. "Proceed, Doctor Egg."

"Gold will be cracked," Petulus said. "'Cracked crown' is a common saying."

A crown is a coin (or a head). A crown that developed a crack that penetrated a circle near the edge of the coin was no longer legal tender.

"Aye, that's a broken head," Pipenetta said.

A crown is the top of a head.

"Nay, then I see thou have a broken — an imperfect — wit," Petulus said.

"Well, suppose gold will crack," Licio said.

"So will an egg," Petulus said.

"Go on," Licio said. "Continue."

"An egg is roasted in the fire," Petulus said.

"Well," Pipenetta said.

"So is gold tried in the fire," Petulus said.

Gold can be extracted from ore by being placed in a fire. This is called "trying" the gold.

"Forth," Licio said. "Continue."

"An egg (as physicians say) will make one lusty," Petulus said.

The word "lusty" can mean "vigorous."

"Conclude," Pipenetta said.

"And who does not know that gold will make one frolic?" Petulus asked.

"Pipenetta, this is true, for it is called 'egg,' as a thing that does egg on," Licio said, "and so does gold."

One meaning of "egg" is "incite."

"Let us hear all," Pipenetta said.

"Eggs are poached for a weak stomach; and gold is boiled for a consuming body," Petulus said.

A consuming body is a body that is wasting away.

In this society, physicians sometimes prescribed a solution of gold as medicine.

"Spoken like a physician," Licio said.

"Or a fool out of necessity," Pipenetta said.

"An egg is eaten at one sup, and a portage is lost at one cast," Petulus said.

A "portage" is a Portuguese gold coin better known as a portague.

"One cast" can be 1) one cast of the dice, or 2) one episode of vomiting.

"Concluded like a gambler," Licio said.

"Eggs make custards, and gold makes spoons to eat them," Petulus said.

"A reason dough-baked," Pipenetta said.

"Dough-baked" is imperfectly risen bread, so Pipenetta is saying the result of Petulus' reasoning was poor, as is dough-baked bread.

"The oven of his wit was not thoroughly heated," Licio said.

Petulus' reasoning did not rise to the occasion.

Petulus said, "Only this odds — this difference — I find between money and eggs, which makes me wonder. Why, since there are more pennies in the world than eggs, should one have three eggs for a penny, and not three pence for an egg."

"A wonderful matter! But your wisdom is over-shot — you have missed your target — in your comparison, for eggs have chickens, and gold has none," Pipenetta said.

"Mops, I pity thee!" Petulus said. "Gold has eggs; change an angel into ten shillings, and all those pieces are the angel's eggs."

"Mops" is a term of endearment.

An angel is a gold coin.

Licio said:

"He has put a spoke in your wheel and successfully refuted your criticism, so will thou eat an egg?

"But be quiet, here come our masters.

"Let us shrink aside."

They went to the side, but they could still hear the newcomers' conversation.

Mellacrites, Martius, and Eristus entered the scene. They had been to Bacchus' temple and had consulted Bacchus' oracle.

Mellacrites said:

"It is a short answer, yet a sound answer.

"Bacchus is pithy — full of short but concentrated advice —and he is full of pity."

He read the oracle out loud:

"*In Pactolus go bathe thy wish and thee,*

"*Thy wish the waves shall have, and thou be free.*"

Pactolus is a river in the neighboring country of Lydia.

Martius said:

"I understand no oracles!

"Shall the water turn everything to gold? What then shall become of the fish? Shall King Midas be free from gold? What then shall become of us, of his crown, of our country?

"I don't like these riddles."

Mellacrites said:

"Thou, Martius, are so warlike, that thou would cut off the wish with a sword, not cure it with a medicinal salve.

"The gods, who can give the desires of the heart, can as easily withdraw the torment.

"Suppose that Vulcan the blacksmith god should so temper thy sword, that were thy heart never so valiant and thine arm never so strong, yet thy blade should never draw blood.

"Wouldn't thou wish to have a weaker hand, and a sharper edge?"

Swords are tempered — given strength, by heating and cooling them.

"Yes," Martius said. "I would prefer a weaker arm and a sharper sword to a strong arm and a blunt sword."

Mellacrites said, "If Mars should answer thee thus, 'Go bathe thy sword in water, and wash thy hands in milk, and thy sword shall cleave adamant, and thy heart shall answer the sharpness of thy sword,' wouldn't thou try it and see what happens?"

Adamant is a legendarily hard mineral.

"What else would I do?" Martius asked.

Mellacrites said:

"Then let King Midas believe until he has tested the oracle and let him think that the gods rule as well by giving remedies, as by granting wishes.

"But Eristus is mum."

He was wondering if Eristus had anything to add to the conversation.

"Celia has sealed his mouth," Martius said.

A hawk's eyes could be seeled — sewn shut — as part of its training.

Eristus said:

"Celia has sealed — made an impression of — her face in my heart, which I am no more ashamed to confess, than thou are ashamed to confess that Mars has made a scar in thy face, Martius.

"But let us go in to the king.

"Sir boys, you wait well!"

He was criticizing them for not going into the temple.

"We dared not go to Bacchus, for if I see a grape, my head aches," Petulus said.

"And if I find a cudgel, I'll make your shoulders ache," Eristus said.

"And you, Licio, you wait on yourself," Mellacrites said.

"I cannot choose otherwise, sir. I am always so near myself," Licio said.

"I'll be as near you as your skin presently," Mellacrites said.

In other words: I'll soon beat you.

They exited.

CHAPTER 3

— 3.1 —

King Midas, Mellacrites, Martius, and Eristus talked together.

King Midas was holding the oracle, which he read out loud:

"In Pactolus go bathe thy wish and thee,

"Thy wish the waves shall have, and thou be free."

He said to himself:

"Miserable King Midas, thou were as unadvised and rash in thy wish, as thou were unfortunate in thy wish's outcome.

"O, unquenchable thirst of gold, which turns men's heads to lead, and makes them blockish and stupid ...

"And turns their hearts to iron, and makes them covetous and greedy ...

"And turns their eyes to delight in the view and makes them blind in the use.

"I who did possess mines of gold, could not be contented until my mind were also a mine."

His mind was dark like a mine.

King Midas continued:

"Couldn't the treasure of Phrygia, nor the tributes that Greece paid to Phrygia, nor the mountains in the east, whose guts are gold, satisfy thy mind with gold?

"Ambition eats gold and drinks blood; she climbs so high by other men's heads that she breaks her own neck.

"What should I do with a world of ground, whose body must be content with seven feet of earth after I die?"

King Midas turned his mind to his military conquests:

"And why did I covet to get so many crowns, having myself only one head?

"Those who took small vessels at the sea, I judged to be pirates; and I myself, who suppressed whole fleets, I judged to be a conqueror, as though I might mask the robberies of King Midas under the names of triumphs, and I might call the traffic and trade of other nations treachery.

"Thou have pampered up and engorged thyself with slaughter, as Diomedes did his horses with blood, so unsatiable was thy thirst, so violent was thy sword."

Hercules' eighth labor was to capture the man-eating mares of Diomedes of Thrace. Hercules took a few companions with him during this labor. He captured the horses, but they ate human flesh. While Hercules was fighting Diomedes, Hercules' companion Abderus watched the mares; unfortunately, they attacked and ate him. To avenge the death of Abderus, Hercules fed Diomedes to the mares. Hercules took the mares to Eurystheus, who ordered them to be taken to Mount Olympus and sacrificed to Jupiter. Jupiter did not want such a sacrifice, so he sent wild animals that killed the mares.

King Midas continued:

"Two books I have always carried in my bosom, calling them the dagger and the sword; in which the names of all princes, noblemen, and gentlemen were dedicated to slaughter, or if not (which is worse), they were dedicated to slavery.

"O, my lords, when I remember my cruelties in the district of Lycaonia, my usurping in the district of Getulia, my oppression in the city of Sola, then I find neither mercies in my conquests, nor color — pretext — for my wars, nor reasonable limits in my taxes.

"I have written my laws in blood and made my gods of gold.

"I have caused the mothers' wombs to be their children's tombs, I have caused cradles to swim in blood like boats, and I have caused the temples of the gods to become a stews — a brothel district — for strumpets.

"Haven't I made the sea groan under the number of my ships, and haven't they perished, so that there were not two left to make a plural number?

"Haven't I thrust my subjects into a military camp, like oxen into a cart; having made them slaves by unjust wars, don't I use them now as slaves for all wars?

"Haven't I enticed the subjects of my neighbor princes to destroy their natural kings like moths that eat the cloth in which they were bred, like vipers that gnaw the bowels from which they were born, and like worms that consume the wood in which they were engendered and begotten?"

Vipers were thought to gnaw their way out of their mother.

King Midas continued:

"To what kingdoms haven't I pretended claim as though I had by the gods been created heir apparent to the world, making every trifle a title and making all the territories around me traitors to me."

In order to gain crowns, he would start wars over trifles, and he treated the countries around Phrygia as if they were enemy states. In fact, because of his actions, they were hostile to him.

King Midas continued:

"Why did I wish that all I touched might be gold, except that I thought all men's hearts would be touched with gold and I thought that what policy could not encompass, nor prows, gold might have commanded, and conquered?

"I did mean to make a bridge of gold in that island where all my navy could not make a breach in the island's defenses. Those islands I did long to touch, so that I might turn them to gold, and myself to glory.

'But unhappy King Midas, who himself perishes by the same means that he thought to conquer others: He has now become a shame to the world, a scorn to that petty prince of the island, and to thyself has become a consumption — a destruction.

"A petty prince, King Midas?

"No, I am a scorn to a prince who is protected by the gods, by nature, by his own virtue, and his subjects' obedience.

"Haven't all treasons been discovered by miracle, not counsel? The gods demand that as a right.

"Isn't the country walled with huge waves? Nature claims that.

"Isn't he regarded through the whole world as a wonder for wisdom and temperance? His own strength is that.

"Don't all his subjects (like bees) swarm to preserve the king of bees? Their loyalty maintains that.

"My lords, I faint both for lack of food and lack of grace from the gods. I will go to the river, where if I will be rid of this intolerable disease of gold, I will next shake off that intemperate desire of government, and limit my territories, not by the greatness of my mind — the greatness of my desires — but by the right of my succession."

Martius said:

"I am not a little sorry that because all your highness touches turn to pure gold, therefore all your princely desires should be converted to dross. Does your majesty begin to melt your own crown, you who should combine your own crown with other monarchs' heavy crowns?

"Do you begin to make an enclosure of your mind, and to debate about inheritance, when the sword proclaims you conqueror? If your highness' heart is not tried and tested to be able to defend your kingdom against other countries, every paltry, petty prince will batter it.

"Though you use this garish gold, let your mind be always of steel, and let the sharpest sword decide the right of scepters."

In other words: Let the sword decide who shall rule a kingdom.

"Every little king is a king, and the title consists not in the compass and measure of ground, but in the right of inheritance," King Midas said.

"Aren't conquests good titles to kingdoms?" Martius asked.

"Conquests are great thefts," King Midas said.

"If your highness would be advised by me, then I would rob in order to obtain kingdoms, and if I obtained them, I would be eager to see him who dared call the conqueror a thief," Martius said. "I would dare them to call the conqueror a thief."

King Midas said:

"Martius, thy counsel has shed as much blood as would make another sea. I cannot call it valor, and barbarousness is a word too mild.

"Come, Mellacrites, let us go, and Eristus, you come so that if I obtain mercy from Bacchus, we may offer sacrifice to Bacchus.

"Martius, if you are not disposed to go, dispose of yourself as you will."

"I will humbly attend on your highness, as always hoping to have my hearts' desire, and always hoping that you would have your height of honor," Martius said.

Licio and Petulus talked together.

Motto the barber had cut King Midas' golden beard and taken possession of it, but then Petulus had cheated Motto and taken possession of the golden beard.

"Ah, Licio, a bots on the barber!" Petulus said. "Ever since I cozened — I cheated — him of the golden beard, I have had the toothache."

A bot is a parasitic worm.

"I think Motto has poisoned thy gums," Licio said.

"It is a deadly pain," Petulus said.

"I knew a dog who ran mad because of it," Licio said.

"I believe it, Licio, and thereof it is that they call it a dogged pain," Petulus said. "Thou know I have tried all old women's medicines, and cunning men's charms, but *interim* — in the meantime — my teeth ache."

Dello, the barber's serving-boy, who had been standing nearby, unseen, spoke directly to you, the readers:

"I am glad I have overheard these wags, Petulus and Licio, two mischievous young men, so the barber and I can get revenge for their overhearing us."

Petulus and Licio had apparently overheard Dello and the barber talking about the golden beard, and then Petulus had gotten possession of it.

Dello continued:

"We will take the advantage of them; they shall find us quick barbers.

"I'll tell Motto, my master, and then we will have *quid pro quo*, tit for tat, a tooth for a beard."

Dello exited to tell his master, the barber, that he had overheard Petulus saying that he had a toothache.

Petulus said, "Licio, to make me merry, I ask thee to go forward with and continue the description of thy mistress; thou must begin now at the paps — her breasts."

Licio said:

"Indeed, Petulus, that would be a good beginning for thee, for thou can eat pap — soft baby food — now, because thou can bite nothing else due to your toothache.

"But I am not thinking about those matters.

"If the king were to lose his golden wish, we shall have but a brazen — a brass — court.

"But what became of the beard, Petulus?"

"I have pawned it, for I dared not coin it," Petulus said. "I dared not make coins out of it."

"What do thou pay for the pawning?" Licio asked.

"The interest is twelve pence per pound for the month," Petulus said.

"What for the herbage?" Licio said.

"Herbage" is a pasture.

"It is not at herbage," Petulus said.

"Yes, Petulus, if it is a beard, it must be at herbage, for a beard is a badge — a distinguishing mark — of hair; and a badge of hair is a hair-badge," Licio said.

Motto the barber and Dello entered the scene.

"Dello, thou know King Midas touched his beard, and it was gold," Motto said.

"True," Dello said.

"The pages cozened me of it," Motto said. "They cheated me."

"That's no lie," Dello said.

"I must be revenged," Motto said.

"In good time," Dello said.

Now was a good time.

"Thou know I have taught thee the knacking of the hands, the tickling on a man's hairs, like the tuning of a cittern," Motto said.

"Knacking" is snapping of fingers. Some barbers put on a show as they cut hair.

A cittern was a musical instrument found in barber shops for customers to play.

"True," Dello said.

Motto said, "Besides, I have instructed thee in the phrases of our eloquent occupation, such as:

"'How, sir, will you be trimmed?

"'Will you have your beard like a spade, or a bodkin [sharp and pointed like a dagger]?

"'Will you have a penthouse [bushy mustache] on your upper lip, or an ally [forked beard] on your chin?

"'Will you have a low curl on your head like a bull, or a dangling lock like a spaniel?

"'Will you have your mustachoes sharp at the ends like shoemaker's awls, or hanging down to your mouth like goat's flakes [unplaited locks of hair]?

"'Will you have your love-locks wreathed with a silken twist [silk string], or shaggy to fall on your shoulders?'"

Dello said, "I confess you have taught me *Tullie de Oratore*, the very art of trimming."

Marcus Tullius Cicero wrote *De Oratore*, which is about the art of public speaking.

"Trimming" can mean 1) cutting hair a little shorter, or 2) cheating someone.

Barbers usually talk while cutting hair.

"Well, for all this I desire no more at thy hands than to keep secret the revenge I have prepared for the pages," Motto said.

"O, sir, you know I am a barber, and cannot tittle-tattle, I am one of those whose tongues are swelled and swollen with silence," Dello said.

Of course, barbers are famous talkers.

"Indeed, thou should be no blabbing, because thou are a barber, so therefore be secret," Motto said.

Motto then started to put his plan in action. Dello had overheard that Petulus had a toothache and Motto's revenge would take advantage of that fact.

Motto said loudly so that Petulus and Licio would overhear him, "Wasn't it a good cure, Dello, to ease the toothache and never touch the tooth?"

Touching the tooth would cause it to hurt.

"O master, I warrant — assure you — that he who is your patient for the toothache is patient and able to endure all aches," Dello said.

"I did but rub his gums, and immediately the rheum evaporated," Motto said.

A rheum is a watery discharge; here, the watery discharge is probably tears of pain.

"*Deus bone*, has that word come into the barber's basin?" Licio said.

Licio was surprised that the barber knew a fancy word like "rheum."

By *Deus bone*, Licio meant "Good God."

"Aye, sir, and why not?" Dello said. "My master is a barber and a surgeon."

Barbers could do such things as bleed patients and pull teeth.

Bleeding patients was a medical procedure thought (incorrectly) to help some patients.

"In good time," Licio said.

Petulus said, "O, Motto, I am almost dead with the toothache, all my gums are swollen, and my teeth stand in my head like thorns."

"It may be that it is only the breeding of a beard, and being the first beard, you shall have a hard travail," Motto said.

Petulus was young and just starting to grow — to birth — beard hairs.

"Old fool, do thou think hairs will breed in my teeth?" Petulus asked.

"As likely, sir, for anything I know, as on your chin," Motto said.

"O teeth! O torments!" Petulus said. "O torments! O teeth!"

Motto whispered to Dello, "If I can just touch his teeth, Dello, I'll teach his tongue to tell a tale about what villainy it is to cozen one of a beard, but don't stand close by, for it is likely that when he spits, all his teeth will fly in thy face."

Licio said, "Good Motto, give some ease to Petulus, for when thou were coming in, I overheard of a cure thou had done."

"My teeth!" Petulus said. "I will not have this pain, that's for certain!"

Motto said, "Aye, so you did overhear — and take advantage of — me, when you cheated me of a beard, but I have already forgotten everything."

"My master is mild and merciful," Dello said, "and he is merciful, because he is a barber, for when he has the throat at command, you know he takes revenge only on a silly, weak hair."

Barbers had better be merciful, for they hold sharp razors against customers' throats.

"How is it now, Petulus?" Motto asked. "Do the teeth still ache?"

"Aye, Motto," Petulus said.

"Let me rub your gums with this leaf," Motto said.

Petulus said:

"Do, Motto, and for thy labor I will requite and reward thee."

Under pretense of easing the pain, Motto hurt him.

Petulus complained:

"Get out, rascal! What have thou done? All my nether — lower — teeth are loose, and wag like the keys of a pair of virginals."

Virginals were keyboard musical instruments with a double row of keys. The double row was known as "jacks."

"O sir, if you will, I will sing to them, with your mouth being the instrument," Dello said.

"Do, Dello," Petulus said.

Dello put his fingers in Petulus' mouth, and Petulus bit them.

"Out, villain!" Dello said. "Thou bite. I cannot tune — play — these virginal keys."

"They were the jacks above," Petulus said. "The keys beneath were easy, gentle, and yielding."

His lower teeth were loose.

"A bots on your jacks and jaws, too!" Dello said.

"They were virginals of your master's making," Licio said.

"O my teeth!" Petulus said. "Good Motto, what will ease my pain?

"Nothing in the world, but to let me lay a golden beard against your chin," Motto said.

In other words: Give back to me King Midas' golden beard, and I will ease your pain.

"It is at pawn," Petulus said. "I pawned it."

"You are likely to fetch it out of pawn with your teeth, or go without your teeth," Motto said.

"Motto, withdraw thyself, it may be thou shall draw — pull — my teeth," Petulus said. "Wait for my resolution — my decision."

Motto and Dello retired and allowed Petulus to consult Licio privately.

"A fearful decision, whether it would be better to lose my beard of gold, or my tooth of bone?" Petulus said. "Help me, Licio, to make a decision."

"Your teeth ache, Petulus," Licio said. "Your beard does not."

Of course, he meant the golden beard.

"Aye, but Licio, if I part from my beard, my heart will ache," Petulus said.

"If your tooth is hollow, it must be filled, or pulled out," Licio said, "and the barber will not fill it, without the beard."

"My heart is hollow, too, and nothing can fill it but gold," Petulus said.

"Thou cannot eat food without teeth," Licio said.

"Nor buy food without money," Petulus said.

"Thou may get more gold; if thou lose these teeth, thou cannot get more teeth," Licio said.

"Aye, but the golden beard will last me ten years and keep me in porridge, and then to what use are teeth?" Petulus said.

Porridge is soft food and does not need to be chewed.

"If thou lack teeth, thy tongue will catch cold," Licio said.

"That is true, and it is also true that if I lack money, my whole body may go naked," Petulus said. "But Licio, let the barber have his beard. I will have a trick (with thy help) to get it back again, and a cozenage — a cheat — beyond that, maugre his beard."

"Maugre his beard" means "in spite of whatever he tries to do." Literally, it means, "Oppose/defy his beard."

"That's the best way, both to ease thy pains and to test our wits," Licio said.

"Barber, eleven of my teeth have gone on a jury, to judge whether the beard is thine," Petulus said. "They have chosen my tongue for the foreman, which cries, 'Guilty.'"

Petulus was admitting that he was guilty of taking the golden beard.

"Gilded?" Motto said. "No, boy, all my beard was gold. It was not gilt. I will not be so overmatched and bested."

"You cannot pose — perplex — my master with a beard," Dello said. "Come to his house, and you shall sit upon twenty beards; all his cushions are stuffed with beards."

"Let him go home with thee, ease himself, and thou shall have thy beard," Licio said.

"I am content with that, but I will have the beard in my hand to be sure," Motto said.

"And I will have thy finger in my mouth, to be sure of ease," Petulus said.

"Agreed," Motto said.

"Dello, sing a song to the tune of 'My Teeth Do Ache,'" Petulus said.

"I will," Dello said.

Petulus sang:

"O my teeth! Dear barber, ease me,

"Tongue, tell me, why my teeth disease me,

"O! What will rid me of this pain?"

Motto sang:

"*Some pellitory fetched from Spain.*"

"Pellitory" is a root that was used to treat toothache.

Licio sang:

"*Take mastic else.*"

"Mastic" is a gum or resin that was believed to stop tooth decay.

Petulus sang:

"*Mastic's a patch.*"

A "patch" is a fool.

Petulus continued:

"*Mastic does many a fool's face catch.*"

Many fools' faces are treated with mastic.

Petulus continued:

"*If such a pain should breed the horn,*

"*'Twere [It would be] happy to be cuckolds born.*"

If men were born with horns, they would have no need to get toothache to grow horns (if toothache would grow horns).

Petulus continued:

"*Should beards with such an ache begin,*

"*Each boy to th' bone would scrub his chin.*"

Licio sang:

"*His teeth now ache not.*"

Motto sang:

"*Caper [Dance] then,*

"*And cry up checkered-apron men:*"

Barbers wore checkered aprons.

Motto continued:

"*There is no trade but shaves,*

"*For barbers are trim [excellent] knaves,*

"*Some are in shaving so profound [knowledgeable],*

"*By tricks they shave [cheat] a kingdom round.*"

Sophronia, Celia, Camilla, Amerula, and Suavia talked together.

Sophronia was the daughter of King Midas, and Celia was the daughter of Mellacrites.

Camilla, Amerula, and Suavia were ladies of the court.

Sophronia said, "Ladies, here we must await the happy return of my father, but in the meantime, what pastime shall we use to pass the time? I will agree to any, as long as it is not to talk about love."

"Then sleep is the best exercise," Suavia said.

"Why, Suavia, are you so light that you must chat about love, or are you so heavy that you must sleep?" Sophronia asked.

"Light" can mean 1) frivolous, or 2) wanton.

"Heavy" means "tired" in this context.

Sophronia continued:

"Penelope in the absence of her lord beguiled the days with spinning."

In Homer's *Odyssey*, Odysseus, Penelope's husband, was away from home for twenty years. He fought in the Trojan War for ten years, and then it took ten more years for him to return home. Much of that time, he was kept prisoner on an island by the goddess Calypso. Because people thought that Odysseus was dead, over one hundred suitors tried to convince Penelope to marry one of them. Penelope was able to hold off the suitors with her famous weaving trick. She said that she would marry one of the suitors after she had finished weaving a shroud for Odysseus' aged father. Each day she wove the shroud, and each night she unwove what she had woven.

Suavia said, "Indeed she spun a fair thread, as if it were to make a string to the bow wherein she drew her wooers."

Eventually, Penelope was caught unweaving what she had women, and she then said that she would marry whichever suitor could string Odysseus' bow and shoot an arrow through the holes in the heads of twelve axes lined up in a row.

Sophronia said, "Why, Suavia, it was a bow that she knew to be above their strength, and therein she showed her wit."

Yes, Penelope was intelligent. None of the suitors was strong enough to string Odysseus' bow.

Suavia said, "*Qui latus arguerit corneus arcus erat*: It was made of horn, madam, and therein she showed her meaning."

The Latin means: "A bow of horn proved his strength."

Suavia was being playful. In this society, people joked about the invisible horns on the heads of cuckolds: husbands with unfaithful wives. She was hinting that Penelope wanted to sleep with or had slept with the suitors.

"Why, don't thou think she was chaste?" Sophronia asked.

"Yes, by all her wooers," Suavia said.

In other words: Yes, she was *chased* by all her wooers.

Sophronia said:

"To talk with thee, Suavia, is to lose time, not to spend it well.

"What do you say, Amerula? What shall we do?"

"Tell tales," Amerula answered.

"What do you say, Celia?" Sophronia asked.

"Sing," Celia answered.

"What do you think, Camilla?" Sophronia asked.

"Dance," Camilla answered.

Sophronia said, "You see, Suavia, that there are other things to keep one from idleness, besides love. Indeed, there is nothing to make idleness, except love."

"Well, let me stand aside and feed my own thoughts with sweetness, while the other women fill your eyes and ears with songs and dancings," Suavia said.

"Amerula, begin thy tale," Sophronia said.

Amerula began:

"There dwelt formerly in Phrygia a lady who was very fair and pretty, but who was surpassingly froward and ungovernable, as much marveled at for beauty, as misliked for peevishness. High she was in the instep, but short in the heel; she was straitlaced, but loose bodied."

"High in the instep" means that she was proud.

"Straitlaced" means that she was stiff in manner.

"Short in the heel" and "loose bodied" both mean "unchaste and "wanton."

Amerula continued:

"It came to pass that a gentleman, as young in wit and in intelligence as in years, and in years truly a boy, chanced to glance his eyes on her, and there they were dazzled by her beauty like larks that are caught in the sun with the glittering of a glass, aka mirror.

"In her fair looks were his thoughts entangled, like the birds of the Canary Islands that fall into a silken net.

"Dote he did without measure and limit, and die he must without her love.

"She, on the other side, as one who knew what was good for her, began to look askance — look at him with disapproval — and yet she felt the passions of love eating into her heart, though she dissembled her feelings of love with her eyes."

Suavia laughed.

"Why do thou laugh?" Sophronia asked.

Suavia answered:

"I laugh to see you, madam, so tame as to be brought to hear a tale of love, who before were so wild you would not come to speak the name of love.

"And I laugh because Amerula could devise how to spend the time with a tale, with the only stipulation being that she might not talk of love, and now she makes love the sole subject of her tale."

Sophronia said:

"Indeed, I was overshot — I missed the mark — in judgment, and she missed the mark in discretion.

"Amerula, another tale or none; this tale is too much about love."

Suavia said:

"Nay, let me hear any woman tell a tale of ten lines long without it tending towards love, and I will be bound never to go to the court.

"And you, Camilla, who would like to trip — to dance — on your pettitoes — your little toes — can you persuade me to take delight to dance, and not love? Or can you persuade me that you, who cannot rule your feet, can guide your affections and your love, having the one [affections and love] be as unstaid and unrestrained as the other [feet] are unsteady. Dancing is love's sauce; therefore, I dare to be so saucy, if you love to dance, as to say you dance for love.

"But Celia, she will sing, whose voice if it should utter her thoughts, would make the tune of a heart out of tune. She who has crotchets [musical notes] in her head also has love conceits [love notions]. I dare swear she harps not only on plain song."

"Plain song" is unaccompanied song. Celia is supposed to harp on plain song, and so she accompanies the song. "Plain song" is here meant to refer to the state of being single. "Plain song with harp accompaniment" is intended here to refer to a love couple.

Suavia continued:

"And, Sophronia, none of them use plain dealing in front of you, but because they see you so curious — so squeamish — to talk above love, they frame themselves counterfeit."

In other words: They are eager to talk about love, but because you are squeamish, they pretend that they are not eager to talk about love.

Suavia continued:

"As for myself, as I know honest love to be a thing inseparable from our sex, so I think it most allowable in the royal court, unless we would have all our thoughts made of churchwork and charity, and so carry a holy face, and a hollow heart."

Suavia was honest in talking about her beliefs concerning love.

"Ladies, how do you like Suavia in her loving vein?" Sophronia asked.

"We are content at this time to soothe — to humor — her in her vanity," Celia said, punning on vain/vein.

"She casts all our minds in the mold of her own head, and yet she errs as far from our meanings, as she does from her own modesty," Amerula said.

Suavia said:

"Amerula, if you were not bitter, your name would have been ill bestowed."

The name "Amerula" comes from the Latin word *amarus*, which means "bitter."

Suavia continued:

"But I think it as lawful in the royal court to be accounted both loving and chaste, as you think it lawful in the temple to seem religious, and actually be spiteful."

Camilla said, "I wonder if you will reply any more, Amerula, because Suavia's tongue is so nimble it will never lie still."

"My tongue is much like thy feet, Camilla, which were taught not to stand still," Suavia said.

Sophronia said:

"So, no more, ladies. Let our coming to sport not turn to spite.

"Suavia, love if thou think it sweet.

"Celia, sing for thine own content.

"Amerula, tell tales.

"And Camilla, dance.

"And so, with everyone engaging in her own delight, no one shall have cause to be discontent.

"But here comes Martius and the rest."

Martius, Mellacrites, and others entered the scene.

Sophronia asked:

"What is the news, Martius, about my sovereign and father King Midas?"

Martius answered:

"Madame, he had no sooner bathed his limbs in the river, but it turned into a golden stream, the sands turned into fine gold, and all turned to gold that was cast into the water.

"King Midas, dismayed at the sudden alteration, assayed again to touch a stone, but he could not alter the nature of the stone.

"Then we went with him to the temple of Bacchus, where we made offerings of a lance wreathed about with ivy, garlands of ripe grapes, and skins of wolves and panthers, and a great standing cup of the water that so lately was turned to gold.

"Bacchus accepted our gifts, and he commanded King Midas to honor the gods, and also he wished King Midas to be as wise as he meant to have made King Midas fortunate."

Sophronia said:

"Happy Sophronia, thou have lived to hear this good news, and happy King Midas, if thou live better to better govern thy fortune.

"But what has become of our king?"

Mellacrites said:

"King Midas, overjoyed with this good fortune, decided to take some solace in the woods, where we roused a great boar by chance. King Midas, eager in the sport, outrode us; and we, thinking he had come to his palace some other way, came ourselves the shortest and quickest way.

"If he has not yet returned, he cannot be long in returning.

"We have also lost our pages, who we think are with him."

Sophronia said:

"May the gods shield him from all harms. The woods are full of tigers, and he is full of courage. Wild beasts make no distinction between a king and a countryman; nor do hunters in the heat of their pastime fear the fierceness of the boar more than they fear the fearfulness of the hare.

"But I hope all is well. Let us go in to see all is well."

CHAPTER 4

— 4.1 —

Apollo, Pan, the nymph Erato, and some other nymphs met in a glade in the forest on Mount Tmolus, which is located in the country of Lydia, which neighbored the country of Phrygia. A glade is an open area in a wood.

Erato was a priestess of Pan.

Apollo is the god of music, archery, medicine, and more.

Pan is the god of the wild, and he is a companion to the nymphs. Shepherds worship him. Pan's lower half is a goat, and his top half is mostly human although he has the horns of a goat.

Apollo and Pan were about to engage in a contest of musical skill.

Apollo said:

"Pan, will thou contend with Apollo, who tunes the heavens, and makes them all hang by harmony?

"Orpheus, who caused trees to move with the sweetness of his harp, offers yearly homage to my lute.

"So does Arion, who brought dolphins to his sugared notes; and so does Amphion, who by music reared the walls of Thebes."

Orpheus could tame wild beasts with his music, and his music once caused the trees of Mount Olympus to follow him.

Arion's music won him many valuable prizes. When he sailed home after winning some prizes, the sailors planned to murder him and take his prizes. Before the sailors threw Arion into the sea, they allowed him to play music. The music, which was in praise of Apollo, attracted the attention of some music-loving dolphins, and when Arion was thrown into the sea, a dolphin allowed Arion to ride him and took him safely to shore.

According to mythology, twin brothers built the stone walls of Thebes. Zethus carried the stones, while Amphion played his lyre, a musical instrument, and stones rose in the air and floated to where they fit in the wall.

Apollo continued:

"Only Pan with his harsh whistle (which makes beasts shake for fear, not men dance for joy) seeks to compare with Apollo."

Pan invented the shepherd's flute as well as the pan flute. The pan flute is also known as panpipes and as a syrinx.

Pan said:

"Pan is a god, and Apollo is no more. Comparisons cannot be odious, where the deities are equal. This pipe (my sweet pipe) was once a nymph, a fair nymph, who was once my lovely mistress, but who is now my heavenly music."

Pan pursued the nymph Syrinx, who did not want to be pursued. To help her escape the attentions of Pan, her fellow nymphs changed her into a reed. Hearing the wind rustle the reeds, Pan enjoyed the sound, and he used reeds to create a musical instrument.

Pan continued:

"Tell me, Apollo, is there any instrument as sweet to play on as one's mistress? Had thy lute been of bay laurel, and the strings of Daphne's hair, thy tunes might have been compared to my notes, for then Daphne would have added sweetness to thy stroke, and melody to thy thoughts."

The nymph Daphne had been transformed into a bay laurel tree, which became sacred to Apollo.

Apollo said:

"Does Pan talk of the passions of love? Does Pan talk of the passions of divine love?

"O, how that word 'Daphne' wounds Apollo, pronounced by the barbarous mouth of Pan. I fear his breath will blast the fair green, if I don't dazzle his eyes, so that he may not behold it.

"Thy pipe is a nymph? It is some hag rather, haunting these shady groves, and desiring not thy love but the fellowship of such a monster."

Pan was half-goat and part-man.

Apollo continued:

"What god is Pan but the god of beasts, of woods, and of hills? Pan is excluded from heaven, and on earth Pan is not honored."

Pan was not one of the gods who lived on Mount Olympus, as Apollo did. Pan was a god of the wild areas on earth.

Arcadian hunters used to whip a statue of Pan if they were unsuccessful in a hunting trip.

Apollo continued:

"Break thy pipe, or with my sweet lute I will break thy heart. Let not 'love' enter into those savage lips. 'Love' is a word for Jove, for Apollo, for the heavenly gods, whose thoughts are gods, and gods are all love."

Jove is another name for Jupiter, King of the gods.

Pan said:

"Apollo, I told thee before that Pan was a god, I tell thee now again, that Pan is as great a god as Apollo. I had almost said a greater, and because thou shall know I don't worry about you being offended by my thoughts, I now say that I am a greater god than you."

Pan was wrong. Apollo was an Olympian: one of the major gods. Pan was definitely a lesser god compared to Apollo.

Pan continued:

"Pan feels the passions of love deeply engraven in his heart, with as fair nymphs, with as great fortune, as Apollo, as Neptune, as Jove; and none can describe love better than Pan. Not Apollo! Not Neptune! Not Jove!"

Neptune is the god of the sea.

Pan continued:

"My temple is in Arcadia, where they burn continual flames to Pan. In Arcadia is my oracle, where Erato the nymph gives answers for Pan. In Arcadia, the place of love, is the honor of Pan."

Pan was born in Arcadia.

Pan continued:

"Aye, but I am the god of hills. So I am, Apollo! And I am the god of hills so high that I can pry into the juggling — the trickery and the copulating — of the highest gods.

"I am the god of woods! So I am, Apollo! I am the god of woods so thick that thou with thy sunbeams cannot pierce them. I knew Apollo's prying; I knew my own suspicion."

Apollo drove the Sun-chariot across the sun each day.

Pan continued:

"Sun and shadow cheat one another. If thy sun stands still, the shadow is fast at thy heels, Apollo. I am as near to thy love, as thou are to mine. A cart-driver with his whistle and his whip in an ear that can hear truly and with discrimination, moves as much as Phoebus Apollo does with his fiery chariot and winged horses."

He was punning on "moves," which can mean emotionally moves and physically moves.

Pan continued:

"Love-leaves are as good as heavenly nectar for country porridge."

"Love-leaves" are leaves that are supposed to make people fall in love when they eat them.

Nectar is the drink of the gods.

Pan continued:

"Love made Jupiter a goose, and Neptune a swine, and both for love of an earthly mistress."

Pan was deliberately misrepresenting the various forms the shape-shifting Jupiter and Neptune took in order to seduce or rape women and goddesses.

Jupiter became a swan, not a goose, in order to impregnate Leda, who bore Helen, who later became Helen of Troy, and Clytemnestra, who later married and then murdered Agamemnon, leader of the Greek soldiers against Troy in the Trojan War.

Neptune assumed the shape of animals such as a bird, a ram, and a steer in his pursuit of sexual affairs. As far as is known, he never assumed the shape of a swine.

Pan continued:

"What has made Pan, or any god on earth (for gods on earth can change their shapes) turn themselves into another shape for a heavenly goddess?

"Believe me, Apollo, our groves are pleasanter than your heavens, our milkmaids are pleasanter than your goddesses, our rude ditties to a pipe are pleasanter than your sonnets to a lute.

"Here is flat faith *amo, amas*; where you cry, *O utinam amarent vel non amassem*."

Pan believed in plain speech and plain dealing. *Amo amas* is Latin for "I love, you love."

Pan also said that Apollo's love-talk is much more verbose and unhappy. *O utinam amarent vel non amassem* is Latin for "O, if only they had loved, or that I had not loved."

Pan gave the impression in his words that his sex-partners were volunteers, whereas Apollo's sex-partners may not be.

Pan continued:

"I let pass, Apollo, thy hard words, such as calling Pan a 'monster'; which is as much as to call everyone monsters: For Pan is all, while Apollo is only one."

The root-word *pan* means "all."

Pan continued:

"But touch thy strings, and let these nymphs decide."

Apollo said:

"These nymphs shall decide unless thy rude speech has made them deaf. As for any other answer to Pan, take this: It is not fitting for Apollo to answer Pan. Pan is all, and all is Pan; thou are Pan and all, all Pan and tinkerly."

Tinkers mend pans: This is a good skill to know, but it is not an art. Music is an art.

Apollo continued:

"But let's turn to this music, wherein all thy shame shall be seen, and all my skill."

King Midas entered the scene.

"In the chase, I lost all my company, and I missed the game, too," he said. "I think King Midas shall in all things be unfortunate."

"Who is he who talks?" Apollo asked.

"I am King Midas, the unfortunate King of Phrygia," King Midas said.

"To be a king is next to being a god," Apollo said. "Thy fortune is not bad. What is thy folly?"

Since Midas's fortune was good, his problems must be due to his foolishness.

This was true. Bacchus' offer of a gift was fortunate, but King Midas' choice of a gift was foolish.

"My folly was to abuse a god," King Midas said. "I did not treat a god with the honor due to him."

Earlier, King Midas had said about Bacchus, "Tush, he is a drunken god, or else he would not have given so great a gift. Now that it is done, I don't care about anything he can do."

Apollo said:

"That was an ungrateful act by a king.

"But, King Midas, I see that by chance thou have come, or thou have been sent here by some god on purpose. None on the earth can be a better judge of gods than kings. Sit down with these nymphs.

"I am Apollo, and this is Pan; we are both gods. We contend for sovereignty in music. Seeing it happens on earth, we must be judged by those on earth, in which there are none more worthy than kings and nymphs. Therefore, give ear and listen closely, so that thy judgment does not err."

King Midas said, "If gods you are, although I dare wish nothing of gods, being so deeply wounded with wishing, yet let my judgment prevail before these nymphs, if the nymphs and I do not agree in our judgments, because I am a king."

"There must be no condition, but judge, King Midas, and judge, nymphs," Pan said.

"Then thus I begin both my song and my playing," Apollo said.

He sang a song about Daphne and accompanied himself on the lute:

"My Daphne's hair is twisted gold,

"Bright stars a-piece her eyes do hold,

"My Daphne's brow enthrones the graces [and the Graces],"

The three Graces are goddesses of beauty, charm, nature, and other things. The graces are graces in general: mercy, patience, love, etc.

Apollo continued to play and sing:

"My Daphne's beauty stains all [all other] faces [in comparison],

"On Daphne's cheek grow rose and cherry,

"On Daphne's lip a sweeter berry,

"Daphne's snowy hand but touched does melt,

"And then no heavenlier warmth is felt,

"My Daphne's voice tunes all the spheres,"

This society believed that the sun, moon, planets, and stars were encased in crystalline spheres that revolved around the earth and created beautiful music — the music of the spheres — that humans could not hear.

Apollo continued to play and sing:

"My Daphne's music charms all ears.

"Fond [Foolish] am I thus to sing her praise;

"These glories now are turned to bays."

Bay trees are also known as laurel trees. Sometimes the plant is called bay laurel. They are small evergreen trees or large evergreen shrubs.

"O divine Apollo, O sweet harmony of voice and lute!" the nymph Erato said.

"If the god of music would not be above our reach, who would be?" the nymph Thalia said.

"I don't like it," King Midas said.

Pan said:

"Now let me tune — that is, play — my pipes. I cannot pipe and sing, that's a difference in the instruments Apollo and I use, but not in the art. I will pipe and then sing, and then you shall judge both the singing art and the instrument."

Pan first played his pipes and then he sang:

"*Pan's Syrinx was a girl indeed,*

"*Though now she's turned into a reed,*

"*From that dear reed Pan's pipe does come,*

"*A pipe that strikes Apollo dumb;*

"*Nor flute, nor lute, nor cittern [early guitar] can*

"*So chant it, as the pipe of Pan;*

"*Cross-gartered swains, and dairy girls,*"

An out-of-fashion fashion of the time was to wear long garters that crossed each other above and below the knee.

"Swains" are shepherds.

Pan continued to sing:

"*With faces smug [smooth], and round as pearls,*

"*When Pan's shrill pipe begins to play,*

"*With dancing wear out night and day;*

"*The bag-pipe's drone his hum lays by,*

"*When Pan sounds up his minstrelsy [his singing and playing],*

"*His minstrelsy! O base! This quill [a pipe in a pan-pipe]*

"*Which at my mouth with wind I fill,*

"*Puts me in mind, though her I miss,*

"*That still my Syrinx' lips I kiss.*"

"Have thou done, Pan?" Apollo asked. "Have thou finished?"

"Aye, and done well, as I think," Pan said.

"Now, nymphs, what do you say?" Apollo asked.

Erato said:

"We all say that Apollo has showed himself to be both a god, and the god of music.

"Pan has showed himself to be a rude satyr, neither keeping measure [rhythm], nor time; his piping is as far out of tune as his body is out of form."

Pan's lower half was a goat.

Erato continued:

"To thee, divine Apollo, we give the prize and reverence."

"But what does King Midas say?" Apollo asked.

King Midas said:

"I think there's more sweetness in the pipe of Pan than in Apollo's lute; I cannot endure that nice tickling of strings.

"What makes me happy is what would make someone else startle. What a shrillness came into my ears out of that pipe, and what a goodly, splendid noise it made!

"Apollo, I must and do judge that Pan deserves most praise."

Pan said:

"Blessed be King Midas, who is worthy to be a god.

"These girls, whose ears do but itch with daintiness, gave the verdict without weighing the virtue; they have been brought up in chambers with soft music, not where I make the woods ring with my pipe, King Midas."

Apollo said to King Midas, "Wretched, unworthy to be a king, thou shall know what it is to displease Apollo. I will leave thee only the two last letters of thy name, which shall be thy whole name, which if thou cannot guess, touch thine ears, and they shall tell thee."

The last two letters of Midas' name are *a* and *s*, but Apollo was a generous god and added a second *s* to form the word "ass."

King Midas touched his ears, which were now ass' ears, and asked, "What have thou done, Apollo? Put the ears of an ass upon the head of a king?"

"And they are well deserved, when the dullness of an ass is in the ears of a king," Apollo said.

King Midas pleaded, "Help, Pan, or King Midas perishes!"

Pan said, "I cannot undo what Apollo has done, nor give thee any amends, unless to those ears thou will have added these horns."

Pan had the horns of a goat as well as the lower half of a goat.

"The addition of the ass' ears was very good, as it might be hard to judge whether he is more ox or ass," the first nymph said.

Oxen are slow and can be stubborn.

"Farewell, King Midas," Apollo said.

"King Midas, farewell," Pan said.

"I warrant — guarantee — that they are dainty ears, since nothing can please them but Pan's pipe," the second nymph said.

She was sarcastic.

Erato said:

"He has the advantage of all ears, except the mouse; for other than the big-eared mouse there's none as sharp of hearing as the ass.

"Farewell, King Midas."

"King Midas, farewell," the second nymph said.

"Farewell, King Midas," the third nymph said.

The gods and nymphs exited, leaving King Midas by himself.

King Midas said to himself:

"Ah, King Midas! Why wasn't thy whole body metamorphosed, so that there might have been no part left of King Midas? Where shall I shroud this shame? Or how may I be restored to my old shape?

"Apollo is angry. Don't blame Apollo, who is the god of music and whom thou did both dislike and dishonor, preferring the barbarous noise of Pan's pipe before the sweet melody of Apollo's lute.

"If I return to Phrygia, I shall be pointed at. If I live in these woods, savage beasts must be my companions, and what other companions should King Midas hope for than beasts, being of all beasts himself the dullest and stupidest?

"Wouldn't it have been better for thee to have perished by a golden death, than now to lead a beastly life? Thou were unfortunate in thy wish and unwise in thy judgment; thou were first a golden fool, and now thou are a leaden ass.

"What will they say in Lesbos, if by chance this news comes to Lesbos? *If the news comes, King Midas?* Yes, gossip flies as swift as thoughts, gathering wings in the air, and doubling rumors by her own running, insomuch as having here the ears of an ass, it will there be told that all my hairs are ass' ears.

"Then this will be the byword and the gossip:

"Has King Midas, who sought to be monarch of the world, become the mock of the world? Are his golden mines turned into water, as free for everyone who will fetch it, as for himself, who possessed them by wish?

"Ah, poor King Midas! Have his ideas become blockish and doltish, have his counsels become unfortunate, and have his judgments become unskillful?

"Ah, foolish King Midas! It is a just reward for thy pride to grow poor, for thy overweening pride to grow dull and stupid, for thy ambition to grow humble, for thy cruelty to say, *Sisque miser simper, nec sis miserabilis ulli.*"

The Latin means: "May you always be miserable, and may no one pity your miseries."

The Latin quotation is from Ovid, *Ibis*, 117.

King Midas continued:

"But I must seek to cover my shame by art, lest being once revealed to these petty kings of Mysia, Pisidia, and Galatia, they all will join to add to my ears of an ass, which is of all the beasts the dullest, the heart of a sheep, which is of all the beasts the most full of fear, and so cast lots for those kingdoms that I have won with so many lives, and kept with so many envies — so many evils and enmities."

Five shepherds — Menalcas, Coryn, Celthus, Driapon, and Amyntas — talked together in a place where many reeds grew.

"I wonder what the nymphs meant, who sang in the groves, 'King Midas of Phrygia has ass's ears,'" Menalcas said.

"I don't wonder what they meant," Coryn said, "because one of them plainly told me that he had ass' ears."

"Aye, but it is not safe to say it," Celthus said. "King Midas is a great king, and his hands are longer than his ears; therefore, for us who keep sheep, it is wisdom enough to tell sheep."

In addition to its usual meaning of "inform," the word "tell" can mean "count."

In other words: King Midas' ears are long, and he hears what goes on in the kingdom (with the help of spies, no doubt). Also, his hands are longer than his ears, and he can punish those whom he wishes to punish.

Therefore, if the secret of King Midas' ears must be told, it is safest to tell it to sheep.

Driapon said:

"That is true; yet since King Midas has grown so evil as to blemish his diadem — his crown — with blood, his diadem that should glisten with nothing but pity; and since he has grown so miserable — contemptible and miserly — that he made gold his god, gold that was intended and framed to be his slave, many broad — bold and outspoken — speeches and much talk has flown abroad.

"In his own country, they don't hesitate to call him a tyrant, and elsewhere, they don't hesitate to call him a usurper. They flatly say that he eats into other dominions, as the sea eats into the land, not knowing that in swallowing a poor island as big as Lesbos, he may vomit up three territories thrice as big as Phrygia, for what the sea wins in the marsh, it loses in the sand."

"Let me understand you, but speak softly," Amyntas said, "for these reeds may have ears and hear us."

Two proverbs of the time were:

1) "Walls [that is, hedges used as walls] have ears [or eyes]."

2) "Fields have eyes, and woods have ears."

"Suppose that they have, yet they may be without tongues to betray us," Menalcas said.

"Nay, let them have tongues, too," Coryn said. "We have eyes to see that they have none, and therefore if they hear, and speak, they know not from where it comes."

"Well, then this I say, when a lion does degenerate so much from its princely nature that he will borrow from the beasts, I say he is no lion, but a monster," Amyntas said. "He is pieced and put together with the craftiness of the fox, the cruelty of the tiger, the ravening of the wolf, the dissembling of the hyena, and he is also worthy to have the ears of an ass."

Hyenas were thought to be able to sound like a human in order to draw humans out of the safety of a house or other place.

Menalcas said, "He seeks to conquer Lesbos, and like a foolish gambler with a bagful of money of his own, he risks it all to win a groat — a coin of little value — from another person."

"He who fishes for Lesbos must have such a wooden net as all the trees in Phrygia will not serve to make the cod, nor all the woods in Pisidia provide the corks," Coryn said.

The wooden net is a metaphor for a navy. The cod is literally a bag at the bottom of a net. A stone in the cod of the net would keep the bottom of a net sunken. Corks could be attached to the sides of a net to keep them afloat.

Driapon said, "Nay, he means to fish for it with a hook of gold and a bait of gold, and so to strike — to hook — the fish with a pleasing bait that will slide out of an open net."

Apparently, King Midas was planning to bribe officials on Lesbos to help him take control of the island.

Amyntas said:

"Tush! Tush!

"Those islanders on Lesbos are too subtle and cunning to nibble at his trickery, and they are too rich to swallow treasure. If that is his hope, then he may as well dive to the bottom of the sea and bring up an anchor weighing a thousand pounds as plot with his gold to corrupt a people so wise.

"And besides, it is a nation (as I have heard) of very valiant citizens, who are readier to strike than to simply stand guard."

Celthus said:

"More than all this, Amyntas, although we dare not so much as mutter it, the King of Lesbos is such a king that he dazzles the clearest eyes with majesty, daunts the most valiant hearts with courage, and for virtue fills all the world with wonder.

"If beauty goes beyond sight, if confidence goes above valor, and if virtue exceeds miracle and achievement, what is it to be thought but that King Midas goes to undermine and conquer, by the simplicity and ignorance of the man, something that is fastened to a rock, by the providence of the gods."

In other words: The gods supported the King of Lesbos, and they supported Lesbos itself. King Midas was showing his ignorance by attempting to conquer Lesbos.

Menalcas said:

"We poor commoners, who, tasting war, are made to relish nothing but taxes, can do nothing but grieve, to see unlawful things practiced in order to obtain things impossible to obtain.

"All his mines do is just guild his comb, to make it glisten in the wars, and his mines cut the combs of those of us who are forced to follow him in his wars."

A comb is literally a rooster's crest; figuratively, it is a symbol of pride. It can also be the crest at the top of a helmet.

Coryn said:

"Well! That which cannot be changed must be borne, not blamed.

"For my part, if I may enjoy the fleece of my silly — my humble — flock with quietness, I will never care three flocks for his ambition."

"Three flocks" are three tufts of wool, or something of similarly little value.

Menalcas said:

"Let this suffice. We may talk too much, and being overheard, be all undone and ruined. I am so fearful that I think the very reeds bow down, as though they listened to our talk.

"Be quiet. I hear someone coming. Let us go in and meet at a place more suitable than this."

The shepherds exited.

Licio, Petulus, Minutius, and a huntsman talked together in the reedy place.

Minutius was a page; he was small in size.

They would be talking about the jargon — specialized vocabulary — of hunting.

"Isn't hunting a tedious occupation?" Licio asked.

"Aye, and troublesome, for if you call a dog a dog, you are undone and ruined," Petulus said.

"Call a dog a dog" means "to speak plainly in plain English."

"You are both fools!" the huntsman said. "And besides, you are base minded; hunting is for kings, not peasants. Such as you are unworthy to be hounds, much less huntsmen; you don't know when a hound is fleet, fair flewed, and well hanged. You are ignorant of the deepness of a hound's mouth, and the sweetness."

"Fleet" means "fast."

"Fair flewed" means "with large hanging jowls."

"Well hanged" means "with large hanging ears."

"Deepness of a hound's mouth" refers to the deepness of a hound's cries.

"Sweetness" refers to the "music" made by baying hounds.

"Why, I hope, sir, a cur's mouth is no deeper than the sea, nor sweeter than a honeycomb," Minutius said.

"Pretty cockscomb! Excellent fool!" the huntsman said. "A hound will swallow thee as easily as a great pit will swallow a small pebble."

Minutius was small.

"Indeed, hunting would be a pleasant sport, but the dogs make such barking that one cannot hear the hounds cry," Minutius said.

"I'll make thee cry!" the huntsman said. "If I catch thee in the forest, thou shall be leashed."

"Leashed" means "whipped with a leather leash."

"What's that?" Minutius asked.

"Don't thou understand their language?" Licio asked.

"Not I!" Minutius said.

"It is the best calamance in the world, as easily deciphered as the characters in a nutmeg," Petulus said.

"Calamance" figuratively means "double talk." Literally, calamanco is a Flemish checkered cloth made in such a way that the checkered part appears on only one side of the cloth. Only those people seeing that side of the cloth can see the checkers. Similarly, hunting jargon can be understood only by those who know hunting.

A cross-section of a nutmeg shows lines and patterns that have no meaning and so cannot be deciphered.

"Please, speak some hunting language," Minutius said.

"I will," Petulus said.

"But speak in order and correctly, or I'll pay you what you deserve," the huntsman said.

"Go to it, Petulus," Licio said.

"There was a boy leashed on the single because when he was embossed, he took soil," Petulus said

"What's that mean?" Minutius said.

"Why, a boy was beaten on the tail with a leathern thong, because when he foamed at the mouth with running, he went into the water," Petulus said.

The huntsman knew that Petulus was misinterpreting some of the words.

The word "boy" was used to address dogs: "Here, boy!" But in Petulus' sentence it does mean a human boy.

A leash is a leather thong.

A single is the tail of a buck.

"Embossed" refers to a deer foaming at the mouth because has been trying to outrun dogs.

"To take soil" refers to a hunted animal that goes into water as a refuge.

Possibly, there is a hidden indelicate meaning in Petulus' words, given that "emboss" can mean "swell up" or "bulge":

"Why, a boy was beaten on the tail with a leathern thong, because when he [his belly] swelled up, he soiled himself."

"This is worse than fustian — worse than lofty, inflated language!" the huntsman said. "It would be best for you to be mum and not speak! Hunting is an honorable pastime, and for my part I would rather hunt a deer in a park than court a lady in a chamber."

"Give me an English venison pastry for a hunting park and let me shake off — let loose — a whole kennel of teeth for hounds, and then thou shall see a notable champing and chewing," Minutius said. "After that, I will carouse a bowl of wine, and so in the stomach let the venison take soil."

In other words: Instead of a park for hunting, Minutius wanted a venison pie, and instead of a pack of hounds, he wanted lots of teeth. Biting into a venison pie was the kind of "hunting" Minutius preferred. The venison (deer) would "take soil" — go into a pool of liquid — when Minutius drank some wine.

Licio said, "He has laid the plot to be prudent; why, it is pastry crust. An old proverb says, 'Eat enough, and it will make you wise.'"

Petulus said, "Aye, and it will make you eloquent, for you must tipple wine freely: *Et foecundi calices quem non fecere disertum?*"

The Latin means: "Which man has the flowing cups not made eloquent?"

The Latin quotation is from Horace, *Epistles*, I.5.19.

"*Fecere dizardum!*" the huntsman said.

The huntsman had parodied the last two words of Petulus' Latin quotation, replacing *disertum* with *dizardum*.

A "dizzard" is a fool.

The huntsman's "Latin" meant: "They have made him a fool."

The huntsman continued:

"Leave off these trifles, and let us seek out King Midas, whom we lost in the chase."

"I'll guarantee that he has by this time started a covey of bucks, or roused a school of pheasants," Petulus said.

"Covey" is used to refer to fowl, and "school" is used to refer to fish.

"You have spoken treason to two splendid sports: hawking and hunting," the huntsman said. "Thou should say these phrases: start a hare, rouse the deer, spring the partridge."

"Start," "rouse," and "spring" all mean to come from out of cover, but they are used for different kinds of animals.

Petulus said, "I'll warrant that was devised by some country swad, aka bumpkin; who seeing a hare skip up, which made him startle, he soon said he started the hare."

Licio said, "Aye, and some lubber, aka dolt, lying beside a spring, and seeing a partridge come by, said he did spring the partridge."

"Well, remember all this!" the huntsman said.

In other words: Remember how to correctly use these hunting terms.

Petulus said:

"Remember all this? Then we would have good memories, for there are more hunting phrases than thou have hairs!

"But let me see, I ask thee, what's this around thy neck?"

"A bugle," the huntsman said.

"If it had stood on thy head, I would have called it a horn," Petulus said. "Well, it is hard to have one's brows and forehead embroidered with a bugle."

Petulus was joking about the horns of a cuckold.

"But can thou blow it?" Licio asked.

"What else would I do with it?" the huntsman asked.

"But you cannot blow it away," Minutius said.

"No, to blow his horns away would make Boreas out of breath," Petulus said.

Boreas is the god of the north wind.

Petulus was still joking about a cuckold's horns.

"There was good blowing, I'll guarantee, before they came there," Licio said.

"Well, it is a shrewd blow," Petulus said.

The word "blow," of course, can mean a blow with a fist.

The huntsman said:

"Spare your winds in this, or I'll wind your necks together and form a cord — a hangman's noose.

"But be quiet. I heard my master's blast on his horn."

His master was King Midas.

"Some have felt it!" Minutius said.

A blast can be a burst of strong wind, a sounding of a horn, or a burst of angry curses.

The huntsman said:

"Thy mother felt it, when such a flyblow — such a maggot — was buzzed out!"

This was an insult. Minutius was so small that his disappointed father must have spoken words to his wife when Minutius was born.

The huntsman continued:

"But I must be gone. I perceive that King Midas has come."

The huntsman exited.

Licio said:

"Then let's not tarry, for now we shall shave the barber's house."

They would steal stuff from the barber's house.

Licio continued:

"The world will grow full of wiles seeing King Midas has lost his golden wish."

Because King Midas could no longer create new gold by touching things, his citizens would find ways to trick each other out of their wealth.

"I don't care," Minutius said. "My head shall dig devices and my tongue stamp them, as long as my mouth shall be a mint, and my brains a mine."

He was using a mining and coining metaphor that meant that his head would form plans and plots that would make him money, like metal being dug from a mine and then being embossed to make a coin.

"Then help us to cozen and cheat the barber," Licio said.

"The barber shall know every hair of my chin to be as good as a choke-pear for his purse," Minutius said.

A choke-pear is a device that keeps open a person's mouth. Minutius' choke-pear would keep open the barber's wallet.

They exited.

Mellacrites, Martius, and Eristus talked together in the reedy place.

"I marvel why King Midas is so melancholy since his hunting," Eristus said.

Mellacrites said:

"'Melancholy' is a good word to describe King Midas, but if someone else were to act that way, I would call it 'blockishness' or 'stupidity.'

"I cannot tell whether his melancholy is a sourness commonly incident to age, or a severeness particular to the kings of Phrygia, or a suspicion cleaving to great estates, but I think he seems so suspicious of us all and he has become so contentious to all others, that either I must conjecture his wits are not his own, or his intention toward some people is very hard."

Martius said:

"For my part, I neither care nor wonder.

"I see that all his expeditions for wars are laid in water — that is, his plans are suspended. For now, when he should execute his plans and act on them, he begins to consult; and he allows our enemies to bid us good morning at our own doors, to whom we long since might have given the last good night in their own beds."

"The last good night" is death.

Martius continued:

"King Midas wears — I don't know whether for warmth or caprice — a large tiara on his head, as though his head were not heavy enough unless he loaded it with large cushions in his headdress: This is an attire never used (that I could hear of) except by old women, or petty priests."

A tiara is a headdress with a high peak.

Martius continued:

"King Midas' lack of action will make Pisidia wanton and ungovernable, Lycaonia stiff and obstinate, and all his territories wavering in their loyalty to him. King Midas, who has couched and set so many kingdoms in one crown, will have his kingdom scattered into as many crowns as he possesses countries. Each country will once again have its own king.

"I will rouse him up, and if his ears are not ass' ears, I will make them tingle. I am not concerned about my life. I know it is my duty to speak to him frankly, and certainly I dare swear that war is my profession."

Martius was willing to risk King Midas' anger by talking frankly to him, as was his duty, although an angry King Midas could have him killed.

Eristus said, "Martius, we will all join together, and although I have been (as in Phrygia they call it) a brave courtier, that is (as in Phrygia they expound it) a fine lover, yet I now set aside both love and courting, and follow Martius: For never shall it be said, *Bella gerant alij, semper Eristus amet.*

The Latin means: "Let others wage war; may Eristus always love."

The Latin was adapted from Ovid, *Heroides* [*Heroines*], XVII.254.9.

Mellacrites said to Martius, "I, who honored gold as a god and considered all other gods as only lead, will follow Martius, and say, *Vilius argentum est auro, virtutibus aurum.*"

The Latin means: "Silver is of less value than gold; gold is of less value than virtue."

The Latin quotation is from Horace, *Epistles*, I.1.52.

Martius said:

"My lords, I give you thanks, and I am glad, for there are no stouter soldiers in the world than those who are made of lovers, nor any more liberal and generous in wars than they who in peace have been covetous. So then don't be afraid: If courage and coin can prevail, we shall prevail, and besides these things, nothing can prevail but fortune and luck.

"But here comes Sophronia. I will first talk with her."

Sophronia, Camilla, and Amerula entered the scene.

Martius then said to Sophronia:

"Madame, either our king has no ears to hear, or no care to consider, both in what state we stand being his subjects, and what danger he is in being our king.

"Duty is not respected, and courage is contemned and scorned.

"Our king does not at all care about us and his own safety."

Sophronia said:

"Martius, I don't mislike thy plain dealing and plain speaking, but I do pity my father's trance. I must call it a trance, where nature cannot move, nor can counsel, nor music, nor medicine, nor danger, nor death, nor anything.

"But that which makes me most both to sorrow and to wonder, is that music (a mithridate — an antidote — for melancholy) should make him mad, always crying, '*Uno namque modo Pan et Apollo nocent.*'"

The Latin means: "For Pan and Apollo harm in the same way."

Sophronia continued:

"No one has access to him but Motto, as though melancholy were to be shaven with a razor, not cured with a medicine."

The reeds rustled.

Sophronia asked:

"But wait, what noise is this in those reeds?"

"What sound is this?" Mellacrites said. "Who dares to utter what he hears?"

Sophronia said, "I dare to utter what I hear, Mellacrites. The words are plain: 'Midas the king has ass' ears.'"

"This is strange, and yet it must be told to the king," Camilla said.

"So I dare to do, Camilla," Sophronia said, "for it concerns me in duty, and us all in discretion. But let's be quiet and listen more closely."

The reeds made a noise that said, "King Midas of Phrygia has ass' ears."

Eristus said:

"This is monstrous, and it is either an omen of some evil to the king, or an omen of some disaster to the state.

"King Midas of Phrygia has ass' ears? It is impossible!

"Let us speedily go to the king to know what he decides, for to some oracle he must send. Until his majesty is acquainted with this matter, we dare not root out the reeds; he himself must both hear the sound and guess at the reason."

"Unfortunate King Midas!" Sophronia said. "Despite his being so great a king, there has out of the earth sprung so great a shame."

Martius said:

"It may be that his wishing for gold, which is only the dross of the world, is by all the gods accounted foolish, and so revealed out of the earth by the reeds.

"For a king to thirst for gold instead of honor, to prefer heaps of worldly coin before triumphs in warlike conquests, was in my mind no princely mind."

Mellacrites said:

"Let us not debate the cause, but seek to prevent the snares, for in my mind it foretells that which wounds my mind.

"Let us go in."
They exited.

CHAPTER 5

— 5.1 —

Sophronia, Mellacrites, and Martius had talked to King Midas, and he had revealed his secret to them nine days ago.

King Midas, Sophronia, Mellacrites, and Martius now talked together in the reedy place.

King Midas was not wearing his headdress. His ass' ears were visible.

He said, "Sophronia, thou see I have become a shame to the world, and a wonder. My ears glow."

His ears were metaphorically red: People were speaking about him.

King Midas continued:

"My ears? Ah, miserable King Midas! To have such ears as make thy cheeks blush, thy head monstrous, and thy heart desperate?

"Yet in blushing I am impudent and shameless, for I walk in the streets."

For King Midas to walk in the streets wearing his headdress to hide his ears was impudent and shameless: It was the wrong thing to do.

King Midas continued:

"In deformity I seem comely and graceful, for I have left off my tiara."

For King Midas to now not wear his tiara was comely and graceful: It was the right thing to do.

King Midas continued:

"And the heavier my heart is because of grief, the more hope it conceives of recovery."

Sophronia, his daughter, said:

"Dread sovereign and loving sire, there are nine days past, and therefore the wonder is past; there are many years to come, and therefore a remedy is to be hoped for."

A nine day's wonder is something that is talked about for nine days, and then people move on and gossip about something else. Sophronia was telling her father that the worst was already over.

Sophronia continued:

"Although your ears are long, yet there is room left on your head for a diadem — for a crown.

"Although your ears resemble the ears of the dullest beast, yet they should not daunt the spirit of so great a king.

"The gods dally and play with men; kings are no more than men. The gods disgrace kings, lest kings should be thought to be gods. Sacrifice pleases the gods, so if you know by the oracle what god brought about your long ears, you shall by humble submission to that god be released by that god."

"Sophronia, I commend thy care and courage, but let me hear these reeds, so that these loathsome ears may be glutted with the report, and that is as good as a remedy," King Midas said.

Hearing the reeds would be a remedy for pride.

The reeds murmured, "King Midas of Phrygia has ass' ears."

King Midas said:

"'King Midas of Phrygia has ass' ears'?

"So he has, unhappy King Midas. If these reeds sing my shame so loudly, will men whisper it softly? No, all the world already rings of it, and it is as impossible to stop the rumor, as to catch the wind in a net that blows in the air, or to stop the wind of all men's mouths that breathe out air.

"I will go to Apollo, whose oracle must be my judgment, and I fear, my dishonor, because I judged him wrongly and disgraced him, if kings may disgrace gods: And kings do disgrace gods, when kings forget their duties."

Kings' duties include showing obeisance to and respect for the gods.

"What is King Midas saying?" Mellacrites asked.

King Midas had not explained how he had gotten ass' ears.

King Midas responded:

"Nothing, except that Apollo must determine all, or King Midas will see the ruin of all.

"To Apollo I will offer an ivory lute for his sweet harmony, and I will offer berries of bay laurels as black as jet for his love Daphne. And I will offer pure simples [medicinal herbs] for his physic [medicine], and continual incense for his prophesying."

Apollo was the god of music, medicine, and prophecy, and he loved Daphne.

Martius, who was skeptical of oracles, said, "Apollo may reveal some odd riddle, but not give the remedy because I never yet did hear that his oracles were without doubtfulness and ambiguity, nor his remedies without impossibilities. This superstition of yours is able to bring errors among the common sort, not ease to your discontented mind."

Oracles are difficult to understand. Croesus, King of Lydia, wanted to attack Persia, but first he went to the Oracle of Delphi and asked the oracle what would happen if he attacked the mighty Kingdom of Persia. The oracle replied, "A mighty Kingdom will fall." Lydia attacked Persia, and a mighty Kingdom did fall: the mighty Kingdom of Lydia.

When Socrates heard that the Delphic Oracle had said that he was the wisest man in Athens, he tried to prove the oracle wrong. Yes, he discovered that other men had skills that he did not have, but he also discovered that these other men believed that they knew some things that Socrates was able to show that they were mistaken about. Eventually, Socrates decided that the oracle had said that he was the wisest man in Athens because he was aware when he did not know something.

Martius regarded oracles as superstitions. Let the common sort believe in them and misinterpret them, but not kings such as Midas.

King Midas asked, "Don't thou know, Martius, that when Bacchus commanded me to bathe myself in Pactolus, thou thought it a mere mockery, before with thine eyes thou saw the remedy?"

"Aye, Bacchus gave the wish, and therefore was likely also to give the remedy," Martius said.

King Midas said:

"And who knows whether Apollo gave me these ears, and therefore may release the punishment?"

King Midas had not told the others that it was Apollo who had given him ass' ears, and he had not told them why Apollo had done that. He was keeping his mistaken judgment about Apollo's musical ability secret.

He was ashamed of that more than he was ashamed of his ass' ears.

King Midas continued:

"Well, don't reply, for I will go to Delphos."

He meant the oracle at Delphi, which was named after Apollo's son Delphos.

King Midas continued:

"In the meantime, let it be proclaimed that if there are any so cunning that they can tell the reason of these reeds creaking, he shall have my daughter to be his wife, or if she should refuse it, a dukedom for his pains, and in addition, that whosoever is so bold as to say that King Midas has ass' ears shall immediately lose his own ears."

The cropping of ears — cutting off the ears — was a punishment in Elizabethan England.

"Dear father, then go forwards, prepare for the sacrifice, and dispose of Sophronia as it best pleases you," Sophronia said.

She was willing to marry whoever her father told her to marry.

"Come, let us go in," King Midas said.

They exited.

Licio and Petulus talked together in the gardens before the palace.

They had been busy. Motto the barber had cured Petulus' toothache after getting the promise that they would return the golden beard they had stolen from him. The pawnbroker had given back the golden beard, which was now in Motto the barber's possession, but the pawnbroker had wanted a list of Motto's possessions that would serve as security. Licio and Petulus now planned to divide Motto's possessions between themselves.

"What a rascal Motto was to cozen and cheat us and say there were thirty men in a room that would undo and ruin us, and when all came to all, they were only table-men," Petulus said.

Table-men are the pieces in a chess game.

Apparently, Motto had said that if Licio and Petulus did not give him the golden beard, he had men in the next room who would beat them up.

"Aye," Licio said, "and then to give us an inventory of all his goods, only to redeem the beard! But we will be even with him, and I'll be forsworn unless I'll be revenged.

Petulus said, "And here I vow by my concealed beard, if ever it chances to be discovered to the world, that it may make a pike-devant. I will have it so sharp pointed that it shall stab Motto like a poignado."

His beard was concealed because he had not yet grown a beard.

A pique-devant is a short, pointed beard.

A pike is a long-handled weapon with a pointed end.

A poignado is a dagger.

Licio said:

"And I protest by these hairs on my head, which are just casualties and things subject to chance — for alas, who doesn't know how soon they are lost. Autumn shaves like a razor."

Yes, men in the autumn of their lives sometimes begin to go bald.

Licio continued:

"If these locks of hair are rooted against wind and weather, spring and fall, I swear they shall not be lopped until Motto by my knavery becomes so bald that I may write verses on his scalp. In witness whereof I eat this hair."

He ate a hair.

Licio continued:

"Now must thou, Petulus, kiss thy beard, for that was the book — the Bible — thou swear by."

Petulus said:

"Nay, I wish I could come but to kiss my chin, which is as yet the cover of my book!"

Petulus had not yet grown a beard.

Petulus continued:

"But my word shall stand. I give my word that I will be revenged. Now let us read the inventory of Motto's possessions. We'll share them equally."

"What else?" Licio said.

Petulus began to read the inventory out loud:

"*An inventory of all Motto's moveable bads and goods, as also of such debts as are owing him, with such household stuff as cannot be removed.*"

"Bads" are goods of poor quality.

Petulus continued to read the inventory out loud:

"*Imprimis, in the bed-chamber, one foul wife, and five small children.*"

Imprimis means "in the first place."

"I'll not share in that," Licio said.

"I am content — thou can take them all," Petulus said. "These are his moveable bads."

Licio meant that he didn't want any of these things, but Petulus pretended that Licio meant that he didn't want to share possession of any of them.

"And from me they shall be removeables," Licio said.

He wanted these items to be far removed from him.

Petulus continued to read the inventory out loud:

"*Item, in the servant's chamber, two pair of curst queans' tongues.*"

"Queans" are "scolds" or "strumpets."

"Tongs thou would say," Licio said.

"Nay, the tongues of queans pinch worse than tongs," Petulus said.

"I'll guarantee that they are moveables," Licio said.

Scolds' tongues are moveable items, for they are constantly moving.

Petulus continued to read the inventory out loud:

"*Item, one pair of horns in the bride-chamber, on the bed's head.*"

"The beast's head, for Motto is stuffed with horns in the head, and these are among unmoveable goods," Licio said.

Licio was again joking that Motto the barber was a cuckold.

Petulus said, "Well, *Felix quem faciunt aliena pericula cautum.*"

He then translated the Latin: "Happy are they whom other men's *homes* do make to beware."

His translation was a little off. The correct translation is this: "Happy are they whom other men's *harms* do make to beware."

Petulus continued to read the inventory out loud:

"*Item, a broken pate — head — owed to me by a member of the Cole household, for notching his head like a chessboard.*"

"Take thou that, and I give thee all the rest of his debts," Licio said.

He made a motion as if he were going to strike Petulus.

"*Noli me tangere,*" Petulus said.

The Latin means: "Don't touch me."

Petulus then said, "I refuse the executorship because I will not meddle with his desperate debts."

Petulus continued to read the inventory out loud:

"*Item, a hundred shrewd turns owed to me by the pages in the court, because I will not trust them for trimming.*"

"Shrewd turns" are "bad deeds."

"Trimming" means "cheating."

"That's due debt," Licio said.

"Well, because Motto is poor, they shall be paid to him *cum recumbentibus,*" Petulus said.

"*Cum recumbentibus*" means "with interest."

Petulus continued:

"*All the pages shall enter into recognizance.*"

According to the *Oxford English Dictionary*, "recognizance" means "A bond or obligation by which a person undertakes before a court or magistrate to perform some act or observe some condition, such as to pay a debt, or appear when summoned; the action or process of entering such a bond."

Petulus then said:

"But *ecce*, Pipenetta sings it."

The Latin *ecce* means "behold."

Pipenetta entered the scene, singing a song about virginity:

1. *"'Las! [Alas!] How long shall I*

"And my maidenhead [virginity] lie

"In a cold bed all the night long,

"I cannot abide it,

"Yet away cannot chide it,

"Though I find it does me some wrong.

2. *"Can anyone tell*

"Where this fine thing doth [does] dwell,

"That carries nor [neither] form nor fashion?

"It both heats and cools,

"'Tis [It is] a bauble [trifle] for fools,

"Yet catched at [sought] in every nation.

3. *"Say a maid were so crossed [thwarted],*

"As to see this toy [trifle] lost,

"Cannot hue and cry fetch it again?"

A hue and cry is a pursuit after a thief. The victim cries out, and citizens who hear the victim are obliged to run in pursuit of the thief.

"'Las! [Alas!] No, for 'tis [it is] driven

"Nor [Neither] to hell, nor to Heaven,

"When 'tis [it is] found, 'tis [it is] lost even then."

Pipenetta then said:

"Hey ho! I wish that I were a witch, so that I might be a duchess."

King Midas had offered either marriage to his daughter or a duchy to whoever solved the riddle of why the reeds were saying, "Midas the king has ass' ears."

A witch might be able to cast a spell and solve the riddle.

Petulus said:

"I don't know whether thy fortune is to be a duchess, but I am sure thy face serves thee well for a witch.

"What's the matter? What's going on?"

"The matter?" Pipenetta said. "By the Virgin Mary, it is proclaimed that whosoever can tell the cause of the reeds' song shall either have Sophronia to wife, or (if she refuses to marry) a dukedom for his wisdom. Besides that, it is proclaimed that whosoever says that King Midas has ass' ears shall lose their ears."

Licio said:

"I'll be a duke, I find honor to bud in my head, and I think every joint of my arms, from the shoulder to the little finger, says, 'Send for the herald.'"

Heralds make proclamations, such as: "Licio is the new duke!"

Licio continued:

"My coat of arms is all armory, aka a place for arms. They are all gules, sables, azure, or vert, pur, post, pair, etc."

Some of these terms are real heraldic colors that can be used in a coat of arms:

Gules = red, *sables* = black, *azure* = blue, and *vert* = green.

Post and pair is the name of a card game, and *pur* is the name of a jack in that game.

Petulus said:

"And my heart is like a hearth where Cupid is making a fire, for Sophronia shall be my wife.

"I think Venus and Nature stand, with each of them using a pair of bellows, the one cooling my low birth to make it evaporate away, and the other kindling my lofty affections."

"Apollo will help me because I can sing," Pipenetta said.

Apollo is a god of song.

"Mercury will help me because I can lie," Licio said.

Mercury is the god of thieves. He was born in the morning, he invented and played the lyre around noon, and he stole Apollo's cattle in the evening.

Petulus said:

"All the gods will help me because I can lie, sing, swear, and love.

"But quiet, here comes Motto. Now we shall have a fit time to be revenged, if by a trick we can make him say, 'King Midas has ass' ears.'"

If Motto were to say, "King Midas has ass' ears," he would be in danger of having his own ears cut off.

Motto and Dello entered the scene.

"Let us not seem to be angry about the inventory, and you shall see my wit to be the hangman for his tongue," Licio said.

Licio will use his wit and intelligence to attempt to trick Motto into saying the forbidden words.

"Why, fools, does a barber have a tongue?" Pipenetta asked.

She was joking that barbers are NOT known for being talkative.

"We'll make him have a tongue, and his teeth that look like a comb shall be the scissors to cut it off," Petulus said.

"Please let me have the odd ends: his cut-off tongue," Pipenetta said. "I fear nothing as much as to be tongue-tied."

Licio said, "Thou shall have all the shavings, and then a woman's tongue, which is imped — enlarged — with a barber's tongue, will prove a razor or a razer."

A razer razes — demolishes — something. The walls of some conquered cities are razed to the ground.

Words can cut and demolish.

Petulus asked, "How are thee now, Motto? What! All amort — all dejected?"

"I am as melancholy as a cat," Motto said.

"Melancholy" means "depressed."

Licio, who thought that "melancholy" was a fancy word, said:

"Melancholy? Marry gup! Is 'melancholy' a word for a barber's mouth? Thou should say, 'heavy,' 'dull,' and 'doltish.'"

"Marry gup!" means, roughly, "Bah!"

Licio continued:

"Melancholy is the crest of courtiers' arms, and now every base companion, being in his mubble-fubbles, says he is melancholy."

A crest is literally a heraldic device at the top of a helmet.

The phrase "mubble-fubbles" means "melancholy" or "depression."

Petulus said:

"Motto, thou should say thou are lumpish. If thou encroach upon our courtly terms, we'll trounce and beat thee.

"Perhaps if thou should spit often, thou would call it 'rheum.' Motto, in men of reputation and credit, it is the rheum; in such mechanical mushrumps, it is a catarrh, a pose, the water-evil, aka disease involving water.

"You would do best to wear a velvet patch on your temples, too."

A "mechanical" is a working man. As an adjective, "mechanical" means "vulgar" or "mean."

A "mushrump" is a mushroom, a fungus that can grow overnight.

Metaphorically, a mushroom is a person who is raised high in society so quickly that the person seems to be an overnight success.

A "pose" is a cold in the head.

A velvet patch is like a beauty mark.

"Velvet" also refers to the soft, downy skin that covers a young deer's growing antlers, and so Petulus is making yet another cuckold joke at Motto's expense.

Motto said to himself:

"What a world it is to see eggs more forward and bolder than cocks! These infants — Petulus, Licio, and Minutius — are as cunning and knowledgeable in diseases, as I who know them all, backward and forward."

Motto said out loud:

"I tell you, boys, it is melancholy that now troubles me."

Dello said, "My master could tickle and delight you by telling you about diseases, and those are old diseases that have continued in his ancestors' bones these three hundred years. He is the last of the family who is left uneaten."

Venereal disease can be passed down in families.

"What do thou mean, Dello?" Motto asked.

Petulus said, "He means you are the last of the stock alive; the worms have eaten the rest."

"A pox on those saucy worms that eat men before they are dead," Dello said.

"Pox" can mean 1) plague, or 2) venereal disease.

Dello was saying, "A plague on venereal disease."

"But tell us, Motto, why thou are sad," Petulus said.

"Because all the court is sad," Motto said.

"Why are they sad in the court?" Licio asked.

"Because the king has a pain in his ears," Motto said.

"Perhaps it is the wens: a swelling," Petulus said.

"It may be, for his ears are swollen very big," Motto said.

Petulus whispered to Licio, "Ten to one Motto knows about the ass' ears."

Licio whispered back:

"If he knows it, we shall hear it, for it is as hard for a barber to keep a secret in his mouth as a burning coal in his hand. Thou shall see me wring it out of him by the use of my wit."

He said out loud:

"Motto, it was told to me that the king will discharge you of your office because you cut his ear when you last trimmed him."

"It is a lie; and yet if I had, he might well spare an inch or two," Motto said.

Petulus whispered to Licio, "It will come out. I feel Motto coming close to blurting it out."

Dello whispered to Motto, "Master, take heed, you will blab all soon; these wags — these mischievous boys — are crafty."

"Let me alone!" Motto cried.

"Why, Motto, what is the difference between the king's ears, and thine?" Licio said.

"As much as between an ass' ears and mine," Motto said.

"O, Motto is modest," Petulus said. "To mitigate the matter, he calls his own ears ass' ears."

"Nay, I mean the king's ears are ass' ears," Motto said.

"Treason! Treason!" Licio cried.

"I warned you, master!" Dello said. "You have made a fair hand — you have gotten yourself into a fine mess — for now you have made your lips into scissors that will cut off your ears."

Card players sometimes drew new cards in the hope of bettering their hand. Here, Dello was sarcastic when he said that Motto had made for himself a fair hand.

Motto cried, "*Perii*! Unless you pity me, Motto is in a pit: He is in a desperate situation."

Perii is Latin for "I am undone and ruined!" or "I have perished!"

"Motto, treason is a worse pain than toothache," Petulus said.

"Now Motto, thou know thine ears are ours to command," Licio said.

"My ears are your servants or handmaids," Motto said.

"Then I will lead my maid by the hand," Petulus said.

He pulled Motto's ears.

"Get out, villain!" Motto cried. "Thou wring my ears too hard."

"Not as hard as he bit me," Dello said.

Petulus had bitten Dello's fingers when Dello wanted to play a tune on Petulus' toothachey teeth.

"Thou see, boy, we are both mortals," Motto said. "I enjoy my ears only *durante placito*; nor do thou enjoy thy finger, except *fauente dento*."

In other words: Dello enjoyed his fingers as long as teeth treated them properly.

"*Durante placito*" is Latin for "during pleasure."

"*Fauente dento* (or *dente*) is Latin for "by the favor of the tooth."

"*Deo favente*" was a common Latin phrase meaning "with God's support." "*Fauente dento*" was a parody of the Latin.

"Yeah, Motto, have thou Latin?" Petulus asked. "Do you know Latin?"

"Alas!" Motto said. "He who has drawn so many teeth, and never asked Latin for a tooth, is ill brought up."

Possibly, "never asked Latin for a tooth" means "never asked in Latin for permission to pull a tooth." Motto's customers included the king and other educated people.

"Well, Motto, let us have the beard, without covin, fraud, or delay, at one entire payment, and thou shall escape a payment," Licio said.

A "covin" is a fraudulent agreement.

The payment would be his ears to King Midas.

Motto replied:

"I swear by scissors, brush, and comb; by basin, balls of soap, and barber's apron; by razor, ear-pick [used to get excess wax out of the ear], and cloths for rubbing faces; and by all the *tria sequuntur triaes* in our secret occupation (for you know it is no blabbing art) that you shall have the beard, in the manner and form following."

"*Tria sequuntur triaes*" means, roughly, "threes follow threes." It may be meant to be a version of "one thing follows another."

Motto continued, describing the manner and form in which Petulus and Licio would get the golden beard:

"You shall have not only the golden beard and every hair (although it is not hair, but gold), but also a dozen beards to stuff two dozen cushions."

"Then they must be big beards," Licio said.

Motto said:

"The beards are half a yard broad, and a nail, three quarters long, and a foot thick, so, sir, you shall find the cushions stuffed enough and soft enough."

A nail is a length of measurement: a sixteenth of a yard, or 2.25 inches.

Motto continued:

"All my mistress' lines that she dries her clothes on are made only of mustachio stuff."

Clotheslines at the time were made of hair. Mustache hair is likely too short to be used for clotheslines.

Motto continued:

"And if I dare to tell the truth, as vigorous as I am here, I lie upon a bed of beards — a bots on their bristles, and they who own them. They are harder than flocks — than tufts of wool!"

Petulus said:

"A fine discourse! Well, Motto, we give thee mercy, but we will not lose the beard.

"Remember now our inventory.

"*Item*, we will not let thee go out of our hands, until we have the beard in our hands."

"Then follow me," Motto said.

They exited.

King Midas, Sophronia, Mellacrites, and Martius talked together at Delphi, in front of Apollo's temple.

He had already made a request for an oracle.

King Midas said:

"This is Delphos: Delphi.

"Sacred Apollo, whose oracles are all divine, although full of doubts because of ambiguity, answer poor King Midas, and pity him."

"I marvel there is no answer," Sophronia said.

King Midas said to himself:

"Foolish King Midas, how can thou ask pity from Apollo, whom thou have so much abused; and why do thou abuse the world, both to seem ignorant in not acknowledging an offence; and to seem impudent, so openly to crave pardon?"

He then said out loud:

"Apollo will not answer, but King Midas must not cease.

"Apollo, divine Apollo, King Midas has ass' ears, yet let pity sink into thine ears, and tell when he shall be free from this shame, or tell what may mitigate his sin?"

Silence.

Martius said:

"Bad! Apollo is tuning his pipes, or he is at barley-break with Daphne, or he is trying on some shepherd's coat, or he is taking the measure of a serpent's skin."

"Barley-break" is a game, somewhat similar to tag, usually played by three couples. Such games can have a sexually titillating element.

At times, Apollo has worked as a shepherd.

Apollo slew a python at Delphi, and he used its skin as a covering for the seat of his oracle: a priestess.

Martius continued:

"If I were King Midas, I would rather cut these ears off close from my head than stand whimpering before such a blind — such an arbitrary — god."

King Midas said:

"Thou are barbarous, not valiant.

"Gods must be entreated, not commanded. Thou would attempt to quench fire with a sword and add to my shame (which is more than any prince can endure) thy rudeness, (which is more than any sensible creature would follow).

"Divine Apollo, what shall become of King Midas? Accept this lute, these berries, these simples [medicinal herbs], these tapers [devotional candles], if Apollo takes any delight in music, in Daphne, in medicine, in eternity."

Devotional candles dedicated to Apollo were supposed to be kept burning for eternity.

Apollo's oracle spoke from inside Apollo's temple.

"When Pan Apollo in music shall excel,"

In properly arranged words (prose has its advantages): When Apollo shall excel Pan in music,

The oracle continued:

"King Midas of Phrygia shall lose his ass' ears;

"Pan did Apollo in music far excel,"

In properly arranged words (prose has its advantages): Apollo did far excel Pan in music,

The Oracle continued:

"Therefore King Midas wears ass' ears:

"Unless he shrink his stretching hand from Lesbos,

"His ears in length, at length shall reach to Delphos."

This oracle was clear: Unless King Midas gave up his plan or attempt to conquer Lesbos, his ears would grow longer and longer until they reached from Phrygia to Delphi.

From the first two lines of the Oracle, those who know how King Midas got his ass' ears will understand what Midas has to do to lose his ass' ears.

Mellacrites said, "It would be good to expound these oracles at a time when the learned men in Phrygia would be assembled; otherwise, the remedy will be as impossible to be had as the cause to be sifted."

He wanted the learned men in Phrygia to hear and interpret the oracle.

Martius said:

"I foresaw some old saw, some old saying, which would be unclear.

"Who would gad about and travel to such gods, who must be honored if they speak without sense, and the oracle marveled at, as though it were above sense?"

King Midas said:

"No more, Martius! I am the most learned in Phrygia to interpret these oracles, and although shame has hitherto caused me to conceal it, now I must unfold it by necessity. Thus, destiny brings me not only to be the cause of all my shame, but also the reporter.

"Thou, Sophronia, and you, my lords, hearken and listen.

"When I had bathed myself in Pactolus, and saw my wish float in the waves, I wished the waves to overflow my body, so melancholy my fortune made me, so mad my folly made me, and yet by hunting I thought to ease my heart. And coming at last to the hill — to Mount — Tmolus, I perceived Apollo and Pan contending for excellency in music. Along with the nymphs' judgment, they also required my judgment.

"I, whom the loss of gold had made discontent, and whom the possessing of gold had made desperate, either dulled with the moods of my weak brain, or deceived by the thickness of my deaf ears, preferred the harsh noise of Pan's pipe before the sweet stroke of Apollo's lute, which caused Phoebus Apollo in justice (as I now confess, and then as I saw in anger) to set these ears on my head, ears that have wrung so many tears from my eyes."

Confessing sin is important in repenting sin.

King Midas continued:

"As for stretching my hands to Lesbos, I find that all the gods have spurned my practices, and those islands scorn them. The gods disdain my pride; men distain my policy: my mines have been emptied by soldiers, my soldiers are destroyed by wars, my wars are without success because they are usurping and overthrowing legitimate rulers; my usurping is without end, because my ambition is above measure.

"I will therefore yield myself to Bacchus and acknowledge my wish to be vanity.

"I will therefore yield myself to Apollo and confess my judgment to be foolish.

"I will therefore yield myself to Mars, and say my wars are unjust.

"I will therefore yield myself to Diana, the virgin goddess of the hunt, and tell her that my affection has been unnatural.

"And, I don't doubt that what a god has done to make me know myself, all the gods will help to undo, so that I may come to myself."

"Is it possible that King Midas should be so overshot in judgment? Has he missed the mark by so much?" Sophronia said to herself. "Unhappy King Midas, whose wits melt with his gold, and whose gold is consumed with his wits."

"What is Sophronia saying to herself?" King Midas asked.

"Nothing, except that since King Midas has confessed his fault to us, he should also acknowledge it to Apollo," Sophronia said.

King Midas said:

"I will, Sophronia.

"Sacred Apollo, things passed cannot be recalled, but they may be repented.

"Behold King Midas not only submitting himself to punishment, but confessing his peevishness, being glad for shame to call peevishness that which indeed was folly. Whatsoever Apollo shall command, King Midas will do."

"Peevishness" and "folly" both mean "foolishness."

Apollo, who was out of sight in his temple, said to King Midas, who was the only person able to hear him:

"Then pay attention, King Midas.

"I accept thy submission and sacrifice, as long as yearly at this temple, thou offer sacrifice in submission. In addition, thou shall take Apollo's counsel and advice, which if thou scorn, thou shall find thy destiny.

"I will not speak in riddles; all shall be plain, because thou are dull; but all shall be certain if thou are obstinate.

"Don't in one balance weigh gold and justice."

One balance has two scales. Gold ought not to make justice, just as might ought not to make right.

Apollo continued:

"With one hand don't wage war and peace.

"Let thy head be glad to have one crown.

"And take care to keep one friend."

Apollo then explained what would happen if Midas did NOT keep that one friend:

"The friend that thou would make thy foe, the kingdom thou would make the world, the hand that thou do arm with force, the gold that thou do think a god, shall conquer, fall, shrink short, be common: with force, with pride, with fear, with trade."

Apollo then gave Midas a decision to make:

"If this thou like, shake off an ass's ears:

"If thou not like this, forever shake an ass's ears."

In an easier-to-understand arrangement of words, Apollo had said:

"The friend that thou would make thy foe shall conquer with force."

Lesbos shall conquer Phrygia.

"The kingdom thou would make the world shall fall with pride."

Phrygia will fall because of King Midas' pride.

"The hand that thou do arm with force shall shrink short with fear."

Phrygia's soldiers shall be afraid.

"The gold that thou do think a god shall be common with trade."

Because of trade, gold shall become so common that it is worthless.

"Apollo will not reply," Sophronia said.

Sophronia and King Midas' other companions had not heard Apollo.

King Midas said:

"It may be, Sophronia, that neither you, nor anyone else, understand Apollo, because none of you have the heart of a king, but my thoughts expound my fortunes, and my fortunes hang upon my thoughts. That great Apollo, who joined to my head ass's ears, has put into my heart a lion's mind.

"I see in obscure shadows that which you cannot discern in fresh colors. Apollo, in the depth of his dark answer, is to me the glistening and sparkling of a bright sun.

"I perceive (and yet not too late) that Lesbos will not be touched by gold, that by force Lesbos cannot be touched, and that the gods have pitched it out of the world, so as not to be controlled by any in the world.

"Although my hand is gold, yet I must not think to span — to stretch it — over the main ocean.

"Although my soldiers are valiant, I must not therefore think that my quarrels are just.

"There is no way to nail the crown of Phrygia fast to my daughter's head, except by letting the crowns of others sit in quiet on theirs."

Martius said, "King Midas!"

King Midas said:

"How dare thou reply, seeing me firmly resolved and decided? Thy counsel has spilt more blood than all my soldiers' lances! Let none be so hardy as to look to cross me.

"Sacred Apollo, if sacrifice yearly at thy temple and submission hourly in my own court, if fulfilling thy counsel, and if correcting my counselors may shake off these ass' ears, I here before thee vow to shake off all envies abroad, and to shake off all tyranny at home."

King Midas' ass' ears fell off.

Sophronia said, "Honored be Apollo! King Midas is restored!"

King Midas said:

"Fortunate King Midas, who feels thy head lightened of dull ears, and who feels thy heart lightened of deadly sorrows.

"Come, my lords, let us repair to our palace, in which Apollo shall have a stately statue erected: Every month we will celebrate there a feast, and every year we will celebrate here a sacrifice.

"Phrygia shall be governed by gods, not men, lest the gods make beasts of men. So, my counsel of war shall not make conquests in their own conceits, nor my counselors in peace make me poor, to enrich themselves.

"So blessed be Apollo, quiet be Lesbos, happy be King Midas, and to begin this celebration, let us sing to Apollo, for nothing can content Apollo as much as music.

They all sang:

"*Sing to Apollo, god of day,*

"*Whose golden beams with morning play,*

"*And make her eyes so brightly shine.*

"*Aurora's face is called divine.*"

Aurora is the goddess of the dawn.

They continued to sing:

"*Sing to Phoebus, and that throne*

"*Of diamonds which he sits upon;*

"*Io, paeans [hymns] let us sing,*"

The sound "Io" is a joyful cry.

They continued to sing:

"To physic's and to poesy's king."
Apollo is the king (god) of physic (medicine) and poesy (poetry).
They continued to sing:
"Crown all his altars with bright fire,
"Laurels bind about his lyre,
"A Daphnean coronet [a crown of bay laurel] for his head,
"The Muses dance about his bed;"
The Muses are goddesses of the arts.
They continued to sing:
"When on his ravishing lute he plays,
"Strew his temple round with bays [a crown of bay laurel].
"Io, paeans let us sing,
"To the glittering Delian king."
Apollo was born on the island of Delos.
They exited.

NOTES
— 1.2 —

"Walk, knave, walk."

The below is from the anonymous poem "A LOOKING-GLASSE O F T H E W O R L D, O R, The Plundred Man in I R E L A N D":

The Parrat, he is learned to talk,
To honest men say, walk knave walk:
But rather then we would do any wrong,
Should cut our tongue if it grow too long.

Source of Above: "A Looking-Glass of the World." 1644.
https://www.luminarium.org/renascence-editions/tract2.html

***

Sir John Harington published fourteen epigrams in Henry Parrot's *Springes for Woodcocks* (1613). The title is *Laquei ridiculosi: or Springes for Woodcocks*, By H.P."

Springes are snares. Woodcocks are proverbially foolish and easily caught birds. *Laquei ridiculosi* means "A ridiculous trap."

The below is from "Henry Parrot's Stolen Feathers":

Sig. K3^v, epigram 31. The phrases were common parrot-talk, corresponding to "Polly wants a cracker." But does the second line indicate that Parrot was actually in prison? Hudibras knew what parrots meant "When they cry Rope, and Walk Knave, walk" (ed. A. R. Waller [Cambridge, 1905], p. 17).

Source of Above: "Henry Parrot's Stolen Feathers." Published online by Cambridge University Press: 02 December 2020.
https://www.cambridge.org/core/journals/pmla/article/abs/henry-parrots-stolen-feathers/26C8C5284288773EC0D711A34AEAB6E3

Note by David Bruce: Paywalls are enemies to scholarship.

***

For Your Information:

> *What Member 'tis of whom they talk,*
> *When they cry, Rope, and walk, knave, walk.*

Source of Above: "Hudibras" (lines 551-552)
https://www.gutenberg.org/ebooks/4937
Note by David Bruce: "Hudibras" is a satiric poem by Samuel Butler. It was written between 1660 and 1680.

***

In Act 4, scene 4 of William Shakespeare's *Comedy of Errors*, Dromio of Ephesus says that parrots have been taught to say "rope."

— 4.3 —

Petulus

There was a boy leash'd on the single, because
when he was embost [embossed], he took soil.

(4.3.26-27)

Source of Above: Lyly, John. *Gallathea and Midas*. Ed. Anne Begor Lancashire. Lincoln, Nebraska: University of Nebraska Press, 1969. P. 138.

Petulus translates his remark:

Why, a boy was beaten on the tail with a leathern thong,
because when he foamed at the mouth with running, he went
into the water.

(4.3.29-31)

Source of Above: Lyly, John. *Gallathea and Midas*. Ed. Anne Begor Lancashire. Lincoln, Nebraska: University of Nebraska Press, 1969. P. 139.

Although Petulus translates his remark, I have to wonder whether there is an indelicate meaning.

The word "emboss" also means "bulge" or "swell out."

Therefore:

Why, a boy was beaten on the tail with a leathern thong,
because when he [his belly] swelled up, he soiled himself.

— 5.2 —

In some versions of the Midas myth, a barber plays a different role than Motto the barber does here.

A barber cut King Midas' hair and so knew about the ass' ears, but of course, the barber was ordered to tell no one about the ass' ears. Barbers are notoriously talkative, and the barber felt the need to speak the secret, so he dug a hole in a reedy area and whispered into the hole, "Midas has ass' ears." Reeds grew in the hole, and when the wind blew through them, the reeds whispered, "Midas has ass' ears." Soon, everyone knew Midas' secret.

In Lyly's play, at the end of 4.2, the reeds overhear the shepherds talking about Midas' ass' ears. At the end of 4.4, Sophronia hears the reeds talking about Midas' ass' ears.

APPENDIX A: FAIR USE

§ 107. Limitations on exclusive rights: Fair use

Release date: 2004-04-30

Notwithstanding the provisions of sections 106 and 106A, the fair use of a copyrighted work, including such use by reproduction in copies or phonorecords or by any other means specified by that section, for purposes such as criticism, comment, news reporting, teaching (including multiple copies for classroom use), scholarship, or research, is not an infringement of copyright. In determining whether the use made of a work in any particular case is a fair use the factors to be considered shall include —

(1) the purpose and character of the use, including whether such use is of a commercial nature or is for nonprofit educational purposes;

(2) the nature of the copyrighted work;

(3) the amount and substantiality of the portion used in relation to the copyrighted work as a whole; and

(4) the effect of the use upon the potential market for or value of the copyrighted work.

The fact that a work is unpublished shall not itself bar a finding of fair use if such finding is made upon consideration of all the above factors.

Source of Fair Use information:

http://www.law.cornell.edu/uscode/17/107.html

APPENDIX B: ABOUT THE AUTHOR

It was a dark and stormy night. Suddenly a cry rang out, and on a hot summer night in 1954, Josephine, wife of Carl Bruce, gave birth to a boy — me. Unfortunately, this young married couple allowed Reuben Saturday, Josephine's brother, to name their first-born. Reuben, aka "The Joker," decided that Bruce was a nice name, so he decided to name me Bruce Bruce. I have gone by my middle name — David — ever since.

Being named Bruce David Bruce hasn't been all bad. Bank tellers remember me very quickly, so I don't often have to show an ID. It can be fun in charades, also. When I was a counselor as a teenager at Camp Echoing Hills in Warsaw, Ohio, a fellow counselor gave the signs for "sounds like" and "two words," then she pointed to a bruise on her leg twice. Bruise Bruise? Oh yeah, Bruce Bruce is the answer!

Uncle Reuben, by the way, gave me a haircut when I was in kindergarten. He cut my hair short and shaved a small bald spot on the back of my head. My mother wouldn't let me go to school until the bald spot grew out again.

Of all my brothers and sisters (six in all), I am the only transplant to Athens, Ohio. I was born in Newark, Ohio, and have lived all around Southeastern Ohio. However, I moved to Athens to go to Ohio University and have never left.

At Ohio U, I never could make up my mind whether to major in English or Philosophy, so I got a bachelor's degree with a double major in both areas, then I added a Master of Arts degree in English and a Master of Arts degree in Philosophy. Yes, I have my MAMA degree.

Currently, and for a long time to come (I eat fruits and veggies), I am spending my retirement writing books such as *Nadia Comaneci: Perfect 10*, *The Funniest People in Comedy*, Homer's *Iliad: A Retelling in Prose*, and *William Shakespeare's* Hamlet: *A Retelling in Prose.*

If all goes well, I will publish one or two books a year for the rest of my life. (On the other hand, a good way to make God laugh is to tell Her your plans.)

By the way, my sister Brenda Kennedy writes romances such as *A New Beginning* and *Shattered Dreams.*

APPENDIX C: SOME BOOKS BY DAVID BRUCE

Retellings of a Classic Work of Literature

Ben Jonson's The Alchemist: *A Retelling*

Ben Jonson's The Arraignment, or Poetaster: *A Retelling*

Ben Jonson's Bartholomew Fair: *A Retelling*

Ben Jonson's The Case is Altered: *A Retelling*

Ben Jonson's Catiline's Conspiracy: *A Retelling*

Ben Jonson's The Devil is an Ass: *A Retelling*

Ben Jonson's Epicene: *A Retelling*

Ben Jonson's Every Man in His Humor: *A Retelling*

Ben Jonson's Every Man Out of His Humor: *A Retelling*

Ben Jonson's The Fountain of Self-Love, or Cynthia's Revels: *A Retelling*

Ben Jonson's The Magnetic Lady, or Humors Reconciled: *A Retelling*

Ben Jonson's The New Inn, or The Light Heart: *A Retelling*

Ben Jonson's Sejanus' Fall: *A Retelling*

Ben Jonson's The Staple of News: *A Retelling*

Ben Jonson's A Tale of a Tub: *A Retelling*

Ben Jonson's Volpone, or the Fox: *A Retelling*

Christopher Marlowe's Complete Plays: Retellings

Christopher Marlowe's Dido, Queen of Carthage: *A Retelling*

Christopher Marlowe's Doctor Faustus: *Retellings of the 1604 A-Text and of the 1616 B-Text*

Christopher Marlowe's Edward II: *A Retelling*

Christopher Marlowe's The Massacre at Paris: *A Retelling*

Christopher Marlowe's The Rich Jew of Malta: *A Retelling*

Christopher Marlowe's Tamburlaine, Parts 1 and 2: *Retellings*

Dante's Divine Comedy: *A Retelling in Prose*

Dante's Inferno: *A Retelling in Prose*

Dante's Purgatory: *A Retelling in Prose*

Dante's Paradise: *A Retelling in Prose*

The Famous Victories of Henry V: *A Retelling*

From the Iliad *to the* Odyssey: *A Retelling in Prose of Quintus of Smyrna's* Posthomerica

George Chapman, Ben Jonson, and John Marston's Eastward Ho! *A Retelling*

George Peele's The Arraignment of Paris: *A Retelling*

George Peele's The Battle of Alcazar: *A Retelling*

George's Peele's David and Bathsheba, and the Tragedy of Absalom: *A Retelling*

George Peele's Edward I: *A Retelling*

George Peele's The Old Wives' Tale: *A Retelling*

George-a-Greene: *A Retelling*

William Shakespeare's 2 Henry IV, aka Henry IV, Part 2: *A Retelling in Prose*

William Shakespeare's 1 Henry VI, aka Henry VI, Part 1: *A Retelling in Prose*

William Shakespeare's 2 Henry VI, aka Henry VI, Part 2: *A Retelling in Prose*

William Shakespeare's 3 Henry VI, aka Henry VI, Part 3: *A Retelling in Prose*

William Shakespeare's All's Well that Ends Well: *A Retelling in Prose*

William Shakespeare's Antony and Cleopatra: *A Retelling in Prose*

William Shakespeare's As You Like It: *A Retelling in Prose*

William Shakespeare's The Comedy of Errors: *A Retelling in Prose*

William Shakespeare's Coriolanus: *A Retelling in Prose*

William Shakespeare's Cymbeline: *A Retelling in Prose*

William Shakespeare's Hamlet: *A Retelling in Prose*

William Shakespeare's Henry V: *A Retelling in Prose*

William Shakespeare's Henry VIII: *A Retelling in Prose*

William Shakespeare's Julius Caesar: *A Retelling in Prose*

William Shakespeare's King John: *A Retelling in Prose*

William Shakespeare's King Lear: *A Retelling in Prose*

William Shakespeare's Love's Labor's Lost: *A Retelling in Prose*

William Shakespeare's Macbeth: *A Retelling in Prose*

William Shakespeare's Measure for Measure: *A Retelling in Prose*

William Shakespeare's The Merchant of Venice: *A Retelling in Prose*

William Shakespeare's The Merry Wives of Windsor: *A Retelling in Prose*

William Shakespeare's A Midsummer Night's Dream: *A Retelling in Prose*

William Shakespeare's Much Ado About Nothing: *A Retelling in Prose*

William Shakespeare's Othello: *A Retelling in Prose*

William Shakespeare's Pericles, Prince of Tyre: *A Retelling in Prose*

William Shakespeare's Richard II: *A Retelling in Prose*

William Shakespeare's Richard III: *A Retelling in Prose*

William Shakespeare's Romeo and Juliet: *A Retelling in Prose*

William Shakespeare's The Taming of the Shrew: *A Retelling in Prose*

William Shakespeare's The Tempest: *A Retelling in Prose*

William Shakespeare's Timon of Athens: *A Retelling in Prose*

William Shakespeare's Titus Andronicus: *A Retelling in Prose*

William Shakespeare's Troilus and Cressida: *A Retelling in Prose*

William Shakespeare's Twelfth Night: *A Retelling in Prose*

William Shakespeare's The Two Gentlemen of Verona: *A Retelling in Prose*

William Shakespeare's The Two Noble Kinsmen: *A Retelling in Prose*

William Shakespeare's The Winter's Tale: *A Retelling in Prose*